"Can we take a piece of pie to *him?*"

Kerri asked.

"Him who?" Quincee teased her daughter. She knew it was natural for a little girl to get a sudden crush on a father figure, but the idea of Judge Hamilton Paxton filling that role for Kerri struck her as hilarious.

Kerri rolled her eyes. "You know, *him.*"

"Oh, *that* him. Sure, honey, why not. But after supper, okay?"

Quincee wondered whether he'd be home, but sure enough, the kids said later that he was, and that he'd handed her back a thank-you note.

Why didn't the blasted man have a Saturday-night date? He was young enough and handsome. And she secretly thought he had the best pair of male eyes in the city....

RUTH SCOFIELD

became serious about writing after she'd raised her children. Until then, she'd concentrated her life on being a June Cleaver-type wife and mother, spent years as a Bible student and teacher for teens and young adults and led a weekly women's prayer group. When she'd made a final wedding dress and her last child had left the nest, she declared to one and all that it was her turn to activate a dream. Thankfully, her husband applauded her decision.

Ruth began school in an old-fashioned rural two-room schoolhouse and grew up in the days before television, giving substance to her notion that she still has one foot in the nineteenth century. However, active involvement with six rambunctious grandchildren has her eagerly looking forward to what this new millennium will bring. After living on the East Coast for years, Ruth and her husband now live in Missouri.

Loving Thy Neighbor
Ruth Scofield

♥ *Love Inspired*®

Published by Steeple Hill Books™

STEEPLE HILL BOOKS

Steeple Hill™

ISBN 0-373-87152-X

LOVING THY NEIGHBOR

Visit us at www.steeplehill.com

Printed in U.S.A.

The second [commandment] is this:
"Love your neighbor as yourself."
There is no greater commandment than this.
—*Mark* 12:31

A joyful heart is good medicine.
—*Proverbs* 17:22a

I can do all things through Him
who gives me strength.
(New International Version)
I can do all things through Christ
who strengthens me.
(Scofield Reference Bible)

—*Philippians* 4:13

To Charles—my own neighborhood boy,
the love of my life.

Prologue

She was in deep muck. Just her luck, lately. Getting another citation for a moving violation, which put more points on her driver's license, came as an impossible complication to her overstretched life just at this time. She hated traffic court. And of all people, now she had to face Judge Hamilton Paxton!

Again.

Those deep eyes of his, his steely gaze had stayed in her memory for days after the last time.

Breathing deeply while she waited, Quincee Davis mentally chanted her motto. *I can do all things through Christ Who strengthens me. I can do all things through Christ....*

Traffic court was a three-day headache no matter which way you cut it. She fervently wished she could simply snap her fingers and make this all go away, but there had been nothing she could do to postpone it.

The court clerk called her name, Quincee J. Davis.

Quincee rose to take her place in front of the bench, keeping her hands still by folding them firmly at her waist, and waited, trying to look alert and interested. After what seemed a very long moment, Judge Paxton turned from his court clerk as he silently accepted her folder. Then he turned his cool gaze toward her.

Recognition flashed in those gray depths with all the warmth of an ice shard in January.

"Miss Davis," he intoned, his voice deeper than the Grand Canyon.

"Yes sir? Er, your honor."

"You were driving sixty-eight miles in a fifty-five mile zone."

"Yes, sir, I was, but—"

"And this is your second speeding violation in less than two months."

"Yes, sir, I know, but you see," she said, imploring for mercy. "I had an emergency."

"An emergency? It seems that I recall you had an emergency the last time you faced me, Miss Davis. Something about taking care of children, wasn't it? Most people arrange their child care without mixing it with constant speeding. You really need to arrange your time better."

"Sir, it really was an emergency. I couldn't leave school on time, and I had to pick up my—"

"Yes, I've heard it before, Miss Davis," the judge interrupted with a bored nod. "Would you offer that same excuse for these parking tickets you have stacked up?''

"Um, well, the parking tickets, while not exactly an emergency, were necessary. You see, one time I had to unload a heavy box, and then my sister—''

"You were halfway into a fire zone, Miss Davis. And did you consider the inconvenience you caused the restaurant by leaving your car in their drive for nearly forty minutes, thereby blocking their vehicles from leaving? Or the neighbors in the apartments whose parking space you repeatedly used without prior authorization?''

Quincee shifted from one foot to the other. She hadn't realized those complaints had caught up with her. Staring at the judge, she noted his well brushed dark hair, flat against his temples. Heavy brows almost met across his brow as he concentrated; his solidly squared chin could hammer with the best of nutcrackers, she thought.

Was it possible to reach a sympathetic soul past those gray depths that were his eyes?

"Your honor, there was a reason for that.'' Quincee put a lot of feeling into her explanation, honest feeling. Heaven knew she had enough of it left over from the last three months. "My sister—''

"That's enough, Miss Davis.'' Judge Paxton's firm tone put an end to her hopes of reaching him on a human level. "I'm sure,'' he continued, "you have enough excuses to fill a stadium. But I've heard one too many. Your irresponsible actions have become a hazard, and you don't appear to have improved your attitude toward getting along with your neighbors in regards to considering their rights and needs as important as your own. Perhaps thirty days without your driving privileges will improve your approach."

Thirty days!

"That's all, Miss Davis."

Impossible! Quincee opened her mouth to protest, her heart beating high in her throat. She couldn't do without her car for thirty days. She had to have the freedom to drive. There was too much to do within the next week, even. She had too many directions to run. Why, she and the kids were moving, for Pete's sake!

"Judge Paxton, I have children to care for. I can't do without my car."

"Then you should think of your children the next time you're speeding, Miss Davis."

"But I must—"

Judge Paxton's glinting expression dared her to make one more protest. He was heartless. She closed her mouth, fighting the flashing anger that wanted to erupt. It was all just too much.

I can do all things through Christ... she began. It had been her hope and promise for the last year. But she didn't feel very capable at the moment. How could she have allowed herself to get those speeding tickets? What was she to do without her driving license?

The court clerk called the next name on his list.

Quincee had no option but to turn and give the clerk all the information he asked for and leave. That or face a contempt of court charge, she supposed.

Judge Paxton had already moved to his next case.

Chapter One

"Quincee..."

The plaintive call came from five-year-old Kerri beyond the opened kitchen door. She and seven-year-old Kyle were in the backyard exploring their new surroundings.

The screen door slammed after Kerri as the child entered the kitchen. "Quincee, you gotta come."

"What is it, Kerri bear?" High on a stepladder, Quincee wiped out the top cupboard. The ancient, once white cupboards hadn't been cleaned in a dog's age, the house sitting empty for the past year after its former occupant had...gone to live elsewhere.

Out of concern for the children, she'd chosen to use that explanation instead of telling them of another death. They were still dealing with the grief of losing their mother.

Quincee had bought the tiny house in this old Independence, Missouri, neighborhood, looking for a measure of security for her and the kids. They'd moved in yesterday. It had cost her every dime of her savings and a borrowed thousand from her friend Laura for closing costs, but it was worth it. Although most of its citizens were older, of grandparenting age, the neighborhood was solid and peaceful.

The house was old, too, built sometime in the early twenties, she thought, and in great need of repair. Too small, really, with only two bedrooms. She and Kerri were sharing. But none of that mattered now. They'd be happy here. She'd see to it.

"That man wants to see you." Kerri's tone was edged. Everything was dramatic to Kerri.

"What man?" She stretched to reach the back top corners, scrubbing vigorously. It might take her the whole morning to get the built-up gunk out, but by gum, she'd have it done and their things put away by lunchtime.

"By the hedge," Kerri said.

Their neighbor, no doubt. The big dusty-blue Victorian on the other side of the hedge, with the long wraparound front porch, had appeared very quiet all last week as she'd come and gone. But most people were home on a Saturday.

"Did he say what he wants?"

"Um, uh, I think Kyle..."

Quincee turned to glance down at her niece. The June sunlight streaming through the door highlighted the moonlight curls around Kerri's face, framing her delicate, vulnerable features. Kerri's wide blue eyes shone with worry. Something really troubled her.

"What is it, sweetie?"

"Um, Kyle and me picked some cherries in that tree back there." Kerri pointed to an unseen spot beyond the visible. "We didn't know we couldn't."

"In the neighbor's yard?"

A slight tremble of Kerri's bottom lip told Quincee what she needed to know.

Quincee climbed down and tossed her dishcloth into the sudsy sink. If the children had done something wrong, she'd apologize and hope to make a friend. She needed all the friends she could get these days.

"All right, let's go," she said calmly. Grabbing a towel to dry her hands, she followed Kerri outside. Whatever this was about, they'd get it straightened out. She planned to build a solid home here, and a good relationship with the neighbors was very much a part of her plan.

Hands shoved into his pockets, Kyle stood against the tall hedge looking fierce. Quincee recognized that look. Kyle always hid his worries and upsets behind a deep frown.

He and Kerri had suffered too many of them this last year.

The ancient privet hedge topped her by half a foot, marking the boundary line between the small property she now owned from the huge yard next door. She surmised it had been planted thirty years before, at least.

Not very tall, Quincee couldn't see over, but she spotted the back of a man's dark head. At the hedge's base, child-size gaps between the old plants positively invited a peek into the world beyond. It wasn't hard for her to imagine the children crawling through, wanting to explore.

She gave Kyle's shoulder a reassuring pat.

"Hello?" she said in her friendliest voice, the one she used to welcome her fifth-grade classroom on a new week of school. "I understand the children have—"

The neighbor turned, his square chin practically sitting on top of the neatly clipped hedge. Quincee stopped speaking abruptly. For the briefest moment, she thought she was hallucinating. Surely, it couldn't be. But it was.

Although unshaven, his dark hair unruly, the man had cool, unforgettable gray eyes.

"Judge Paxton!" Her voice nearly strangled in her throat.

Her first thought was that he looked much younger than he did in his judge's robes. Her second thought was that she was in trouble yet again. She nearly groaned aloud. His scowl expressed a decided unhappiness over a situation she was only now beginning to understand might be a major infraction.

And he had no heart.

His straight brows lowered another quarter of an inch, his nod of recognition a reactionary one. "Miss…Fluff…er, Miss…"

Miss Fluff? He thought of her as Miss Fluff?

Had it been her looks, then, with her strawberry-red hair curling around her face like feathers, or that she'd worn a bright lipstick the day she'd gone to court? Or the misfortune of her driving record?

The resentment from that day in court rose in her chest like a flood.

Quincee straightened and stood as tall as her five feet would let her. She may be small of stature, but she wasn't quite without an authority of her own. Of sorts. At least with children.

She cleared her throat. "Quincee Davis, Judge Paxton."

"Ah, yes. Quincee Davis." He blinked before his face melted into a cool demeanor. "Are you by any chance in charge of these children?"

"Yep." She gathered her forces to answer with in-your-face pride. She would not allow an intimidation of his position to rob her or the children of her protective shield. Whatever they'd done, they were good kids. They didn't normally get into trouble. "They belong to me. This is Kerri and Kyle."

"I see. What are you doing here, may I ask?"

"We just moved into this house."

His jaw tightened as he stared at her in disbelief. "The Denby house?"

"Yes, I bought it. We couldn't move until school was out. I'm a teacher, you see, and though we closed on the house last month, there were too many things to clear up before we could make the move."

She prayed he wouldn't ask her how the move had taken place without her driving here. Or, until she could get around to clearing out the decrepit garage at the rear of the property, who had driven her car, which clearly could be seen parked in the drive.

Hoping to divert that direction of thought, she asked, "Do you live there?"

Actually, she'd been blessed in her move. A number of her teacher friends from school had pitched in to truck hers and the children's few belongings from the old apartment to the house. Although she'd driven her car, as well, piled high with boxes, they'd done it in one clean sweep.

But she'd counted on running errands this afternoon, and buying groceries. What could she do now? She still had three weeks before regaining her driving privileges.

"Yes," the judge answered, his gaze riveted on her. "We includes you, the children and…?"

"Just us." She glanced at Kyle. He hadn't dealt well with his mother's death and he wasn't inclined to use Quincee's softer explanations of what had happened. But Quincee knew Kerri needed the reassurance of knowing where her mother had gone, and so she'd told them what she honestly believed—that Paula now lived in Heaven.

"Yes, we're a team. We do just fine on our own." She finished with a firmness she didn't always feel.

"Oh?" It sounded like a scoff. One of his pronouncements. His jaw hardened, while the gray eyes continued to study her. She almost shivered in their cool depths as he muttered, "I see."

There was no help for it, this was going to be a

difficult neighbor with which to deal. *I can do all things through Him Who strengthens me....*

Quincee took a deep breath and plunged. "Um, Judge Paxton, Kerri said something about picking cherries?"

"That's right. These two were in my cherry tree. I have peach and apple trees, too, in the back corner of my yard. The pie cherries are beginning to ripen. I caught your children eating them right from the tree."

"Kyle? Kerri?" She turned to look at the children. "What do you have to say for yourselves?"

"Nobody else was there," Kyle said, defending himself. "We didn't know they weren't our cherries."

"You must have known, Kyle. They were on my side of the hedge."

"Didn't know it was your yard," Kyle challenged, defiance in the lines of his stance. "We thought they were just there."

"Well, you were trespassing the moment you crawled through the hedge. You must've known that was wrong."

"What's that?" Kyle asked, looking to Quincee for an explanation.

"Going onto someone else's property without being invited," she said to supply the explanation. Both the children's jeans-clad knees were streaked with mud, evidence of their having crawled through the gap in the hedge.

The children had known their limits when they

lived in the apartment. The parks she and Paula had taken them to had been open ground offering pure freedom to run as wide and satisfyingly hard as they wished. A yard of their own was new to them.

"That's right." Judge Paxton pursed his mouth. His steady gaze, not really unkind, Quincee noted with surprise, locked onto the boy's before engaging Kerri's. "And you took something that didn't belong to you. Do either of you think that is right?"

"No, sir." Shame came with Kyle's solid answer, but Quincee could tell he didn't like the embarrassment that came with it. She'd have a quiet talk with him later.

"No, sir." Kerri's eyes began to tear, and her lip trembled.

Quincee's pride in the children rose. She placed her hand on Kerri's head. They may have behaved without thought, but they didn't lie about what they'd done. They understood what it was to tell the truth.

For the first time in her sketchy knowledge of the judge, she heard his voice soften. "Now that we have that out of the way, what do you plan to do about it?"

The children's troubled glances turned her way.

"I'd be glad to pay you for the cherries," Quincee offered. "If you'll tell me what they're worth."

"It's Kyle's and Kerri's debt, don't you think?"

"But they're very young. They didn't intentionally steal the fruit."

"They may be young, Miss Davis, but they're not too young to learn to take responsibility for their actions. As a teacher, I'd think you would agree with that."

"Oh, normally, I would. I do. I agree completely," she was quick to say. "But right at this time it seems..."

His expression hardened, as though he were reminding her of her own recent irresponsibility. Easy excuses, he seemed to say, wouldn't stand with him.

Quincee bit her bottom lip. She couldn't pour out any of her problems to this man, not a one. This man would see any explanation as simply more excuses.

"Well, the children don't have any money." She wouldn't tell him they'd spent their allowance on pizza last night to celebrate their new home. The only alternative had been peanut butter and jam sandwiches. Again.

"I don't want their money," Judge Paxton said firmly.

Lord, "Love thy neighbor" might take a stretch here, Quincee prayed. *Want to give me some help?*

"All right," she conceded. "What will it take to, um, satisfy the debt?"

She didn't like being in debt to anyone. Especially, she was discovering, she didn't want to owe this man anything. It felt too much like the court sentence that hung over her head.

"An apology will do for a start."

"Oh. Of course." She cleared her throat as she felt color creep up her cheeks. She'd been so put off by the fact of who her neighbor was that she'd been remiss in offering the first common decency of an apology. And after she'd thought to be neighborly and smooth away the problem. "Children?"

"I'm sorry." Kerri spoke barely above a whisper.

"Sorry," Kyle mumbled.

"And I apologize, as well, Judge Paxton," Quincee said. "I'll make sure the children…" She let her voice trail as an idea sparked her thoughts in a new direction. "Um, perhaps the children could work off their debt."

The judge glanced at the children once more, seeming to consider the matter with as much gravity as he carried to his position on the bench. "That's a concept. What can they do?"

"Well," she said, glancing at the open denim collar. A few inches of tanned throat showed her he wasn't a stranger to the sun. She wondered how many hours he spent puttering in his yard. She'd noted how neat it always appeared.

She let her gaze drop to the ground. Only the toes of grungy sneakers showed in the hedge's gap. The man couldn't be all poker straight and formal if he could let himself go enough to enjoy puttering in the yard.

"Perhaps they can help you with your yard chores. Say for the rest of this morning?"

The judge weighed the offer, his dark lashes flickering from her to the children. Then he commanded the children's attention. "Kyle. Kerri. Do you agree?"

Kerri nodded eagerly, her face brightening, while Kyle, trying hard not to show any enthusiasm for the idea, spoke for them both. "S'pose so. What do we have ta do?"

It dawned on Quincee that Kyle may be in need of a man's company. He'd been very young when his parents split, and the kids' dad, Mac Stillman, hadn't been seen since shortly after Kerri was born.

"I'm pruning rosebushes against my house right now," the judge said, bringing her thoughts back to the task at hand. "You may gather the clippings for the trash can. After that, I'll be working in the vegetable garden. You may both help with weeding."

Before he'd finished speaking, Kerri was crawling through the gap in the hedge. Kyle scrambled to follow.

Quincee didn't know whether to go with the children or not. They needed to learn this valued lesson, to be sure, but she knew very little about Judge Paxton's personal life. Hamilton Paxton was still practically a stranger, though her real estate woman had told Quincee that her neighbor in the Victorian beauty next to hers lived alone, but was a very respected citizen. The woman hadn't mentioned his name.

At the time, who would've guessed she'd care?

Paula hadn't normally let the children go with someone of whom she knew so little. Neither did Quincee. Yet however much she might think him a stuffed shirt, she instinctively trusted the judge.

"You may check on the children at any time, Miss Davis," the judge said, reading her thoughts. "We'll be right here in plain sight for you to find."

Quincee nodded. His unexpected thoughtfulness struck her as unusual; he certainly hadn't cut her any slack or shown any kindness at court. "Thank you."

Through the low woody hedge gaps, she saw their feet turn away.

"Come home by lunchtime, kids," she called after them. "And you must follow Judge Paxton's instructions, but don't get in his way."

"We will, Quincee," Kerri returned, her voice floating behind her.

"I don't suppose either of you have any work gloves, do you?" she heard the judge mutter. "We'll have to see what I can dig up."

Quincee was left to puzzle over the man's behavior after giving a great imitation of disliking kids. He certainly didn't have much respect for her. He thought her a fluff.

Promptly at noon, the kids came through the back door. Kerri carried a brown paper sack. "Look what I have," she boasted.

"What's that?" Quincee asked.

"Strawberries." Kerri opened the sack and showed off her prize. "They came out of his garden. He said he didn't want any more, he'd had enough. And he let me pick 'em 'cause he showed me how. You only pick just the red ones, see?"

"He gave these to you?" Quincee queried, narrowing her eyes. "Are you sure?"

"Uh-huh. We earned 'em," Kyle said. He displayed more dirt than a gopher.

"And what have you been doing to earn the strawberries?'' she asked. She couldn't imagine what that stiff-necked letter-of-the-law would consider ample work worthy of these lovely strawberries.

"Chopping up dirt and taking out the rocks so the stuff in the garden can grow better," the boy replied. "He said we grow more rocks in Missouri than grass."

"I suppose that's true," she responded with a surprised chuckle. "But I think you both need baths before you grow anything interesting in all that dirt you're sporting. Quickly now, before lunch."

She scooted each of them in and out of a speedy dunking in the stained claw-footed tub, wishing for the efficiency of a shower. It was on her list.

But then, that was the reason she'd been able to buy the house at all, she reminded herself. It had been greatly reduced because it needed so much repair and it was so out of date. She was only surprised the heirs of the former owner hadn't sold the old tub to an antique dealer. One day, she'd have it refinished. That was on her list, as well.

While the kids ate their peanut butter sandwiches, she gently shook the ripe berries into her sink to wash. Only heaven knew where her colander was to be found. Popping a clean berry into her mouth, she closed her eyes and savored the sweet taste.

Sighing, she wondered what to do with all of them. She'd slice a bowl of them for breakfast tomorrow, she decided. Over cereal, they'd be a grand treat. She could make either shortcake or a pie with the rest.

It would have to be a pie, she guessed. She didn't

have enough flour to make shortcake biscuits. And now she couldn't go to the store until her friend Laura had time to take her. One day next week, she thought.

Could she find everything she needed from her boxes to make a pie? She set the children to helping as soon as lunch was over.

Kyle unearthed the baking tins and Kerri found the flour and sugar. Then while the children rested at her insistence, she made a pie crust, praying the old oven would give an even heat. A new stove was on her list, too, but by her calculations she'd have to make do with this one for at least a year.

By the time the kids were up again, the brightly glazed berries gleamed in a reasonably browned crust. She only wished she had some whipped cream to complete her masterpiece.

"Ooh, that looks yummy," Kerri said, eyeing the treat. "Can we take a piece to him?"

"Him who?" Quincee teased. She knew it was natural for a little girl to get a sudden crush on a father figure, but the idea of Judge Paxton filling that role for Kerri struck her as hilarious.

"You know." Kerri rolled her wide eyes. "Him."

"Oh, that him." Well…it was the least she could do, she supposed, to share his generosity in this form. She wasn't about to be in his debt for a single, solitary thing. "Sure, honey, why not. But after supper, okay? And after you and Kyle empty at least three boxes of your clothes into your chests."

About seven, Quincee carefully placed a large

piece of pie in a plastic container and let Kerri and Kyle take it next door. She cautioned them to go around by way of the sidewalk. Would he be home? She couldn't see his garage, placed on the other side of his house, to see if his car was there.

She'd included a note of thanks.

Thirty minutes later, when the children returned, they handed her back the note. At the bottom, she found one sentence added in a short masculine scrawl, telling her the pie was quite good. It was signed H.A. Paxton.

H.A. Paxton. He was a puzzle for sure.

Why didn't the blasted man have a Saturday night date? He was young enough, and handsome.

Well...presentable, anyway. If one liked that old-fashioned kind of man. Why was he home, when most of her single acquaintances joined friends for a movie or a barbecue? Why did the blasted man have to be home when she'd hoped to sneak out and make a grocery run?

But she secretly thought he had the best pair of male eyes in the city of Independence.

Chapter Two

Two afternoons later, Quincee decided she'd made enough headway on the inside of the house. She'd done a thorough inspection of the outdated plumbing and wiring and knew that the wiring must be her first priority in repair.

She'd learn to do it herself, except there were licenses and requirements about those things. But couldn't she do it and then have a licensed electrician inspect the work? That was a plan to ponder—but not until autumn. By autumn she'd have painted the house outside and have a bit of money put by again.

Her long list of needed repairs and updating would take her to her knees, if she let it. "I can do all things through Him Who strengths me," she murmured for the hundredth time. "And I can barter, like Mom used to do."

They would simply have to make do with fans and

one window air-conditioning unit for the summer. The house was as comfortable as she could make it for now. She thought it time to see if the garage was usable.

Besides, she needed another outlet for her frustrations. She'd spent a long, fruitless hour on the phone this morning with the national aluminum siding company that employed the children's dad. Her sister, Paula, had said he traveled from city to city with a crew of men. But the company didn't seem to know if he was an employee or not, nor did they have any idea where he may be found. In this day of the information age, Quincee didn't understand why finding Mac Stillman was so complicated.

Unless he didn't choose to be found, which was probably the case. Paula hadn't pushed the matter, though, saying it wouldn't change anything if they knew where he was. He still would find excuses not to give her any child support.

Quincee hoped that was true; she didn't want to give up raising the kids, and Paula had left behind a notarized letter naming Quincee as legal guardian. But she thought it only right to inform the man that her sister had died and the children were now in her care.

Sadness threatened to descend. She and the kids were still dealing with their loss, nearly four months later. But they'd found solace in each other, and her friend Laura had been a great help. And now their moods had lightened with the exciting adventure of owning a home of their own for the first time.

"I found the hammer," Kyle said, waving the tool. That brought her thoughts back. "Can we do it now?"

"Sure, tiger. Let me change clothes." She eyed his summer shorts. "You two put on some jeans, too. And socks and long-sleeved shirts."

She'd expressly forbidden the children from getting into the old shambles without her supervision. Who knew what they'd find in there? The Realtor had told her the heirs of the former owner hadn't bothered to find out, and no key for it could be found.

Five minutes later, she and the kids marched out to tackle the rusting padlock. She whammed a major whack with her lightweight hammer, but nothing happened. She tried again, setting off nothing more than a rattle.

"Let me try," Kyle said.

"Okay. Couldn't hurt." Quincee handed the child the tool. Sometimes it felt satisfying to hammer at something. An inanimate object. Something that couldn't sustain lasting damage.

"Can I try, too?" Kerri begged.

"Sure 'nuff, Kerri bear. Just be careful not to get your other hand in the way. And Kyle, you step out of her way, too."

Quincee left the kids whacking at the lock to walk around the aging structure. A loud rattle and resounding metallic ring told her they'd hit the wooden doors, giving her a chuckle. If those old carriage-style wooden doors couldn't take the stress, then she may as well count the garage off as a loss, anyway.

She hadn't done more than give the structure a cursory outside look before she bought the place. Probably full of mice, she mused. Oversized, it sat against the back property line a foot from an old chain link fence.

As Quincee squeezed between the back wall and the fence, she caught a flashing sun reflection from the corner of her eye. She glanced over the fence to the tall, narrow house behind hers, spotting a stooped, thin figure with binoculars clamped to his eyes. Waving jauntily, she grinned. A moment later, the old man had disappeared from view.

Quincee chuckled. She sure did have interesting and concerned neighbors.

She continued her examination of her garage. As she traipsed around it, listening to the children's voices float, she decided the old structure wasn't in as bad a shape as she'd thought.

Kyle demanded that Kerri give him the hammer, and an argument ensued. Then, hearing additional grown-up voices, Quincee rounded the corner to see an older couple talking with the children.

"Oh, hello there. I'm Bette Longacre," the woman said. "This is my husband, Gene. We live just across the street, there." She pointed to a large brick bungalow in thirties style directly across from the judge's. Bette had a sweet smile in a plump face and short white hair. "We came over to welcome you and your children to the neighborhood."

"That's nice of you," Quincee responded, smiling in return. She swiped her hand on the back of her jeans and offered to shake while she introduced herself and the children.

The adults agreed on using first names.

"We are trying to open our garage," Quincee explained. "We have no idea what's in there."

"Oh, I can tell you what some of it is," Bette said. "Old furniture. Magazines. Bottles. Junk and more junk. Denby never threw away anything in his life if he could help it."

"Any toys?" Kerri asked hopefully.

"Possible. Never knew with Denby," Gene answered, rubbing his chin. His gaze was speculative behind his gold-rimmed glasses. "He could be a peculiar man sometimes."

"Somethin' going on here?" asked a new arrival. The man who strolled toward them tucked a folded newspaper under his arm as he hitched his baggy shorts over a rounded belly. He had a thick fringe of nondescript hair around his shiny dome of a head.

"Oh, 'lo, Randolf." Bette greeted him tentatively with a quick glance at her husband. "Come meet our new neighbors, Quincee Davis and the children, Kyle and Kerri."

The two men nodded their greetings toward each other rather like two hounds who claimed the same territory. The new arrival turned her way.

"Randolf Bader, ma'am. Saw the commotion an' heard banging," he said. "Thought I should see what all the ruckus was about. Don't have many little kids on the street anymore. Big ones, though. Some of 'em can't be trusted to stay outta trouble."

"Randolf lives two doors down from here," Bette explained to Quincee. "He heads our neighborhood watch program."

"That's good to know," Quincee said. "Well, Mr. Bader, I'm trying to remove this padlock. There doesn't seem to be a key to it, and anyway, it has rusted and corroded until it's completely sealed. So far, a hammer against it hasn't broken it."

"A saw might do it," Gene said.

"I think you should get aholt of one of those tools like giant pliers," said Mr. Bader.

"Don't think so, Randolf," Gene contradicted. "Wouldn't cut it. Besides, those things take a lot of muscle power."

"That let's you out then," Mr. Bader said.

Gene pursed his lips. "And I suppose you could do it?"

"Wasn't saying that, now, was I?"

"You may have to call in a locksmith," Bette said hastily. "They know about these things."

"What's going on?" said the deep voice behind her. Quincee would recognize that voice from only a syllable spoken.

Hearing it certainly caused her tummy to dip. She hadn't heard his approach.

They all turned his way in unison, as though his presence commanded the highest respect even in the neighborhood.

Dressed in a lightweight summer suit, the charcoal shade over a stark white shirt coupled with a cranberry red tie, Judge Hamilton Paxton appeared as appropriate to the law profession as if he waved his degree like a flag.

"Hello, there, Hamilton," Gene greeted. "Just getting acquainted with your new neighbors."

"Is there a problem?" Hamilton asked.

"Not really. It's—" Quincee began.

"She needs a locksmith," Bette said.

"I'm not sure that's necessary yet," Quincee said as she tried again. She didn't want to spend money on locksmith services unless she had no other choice. Her last paycheck had gone to pay for her traffic fine and for the moving expenses, and what little was left had to stretch to the first of next month.

"Old Denby hadn't touched that lock in years," Gene added.

"What would really do it is a sledgehammer," Mr. Bader said. He went to investigate the lock for himself, rattling it as though to shake it off. "You got a sledgehammer in all them tools you got, Gene?"

"I don't want to smash more than the lock," Quincee said hastily.

"Well, I've a hacksaw someplace," Gene said. "If I can find it. M'son borrowed it last winter and I'm not sure it's been returned."

"Please don't bother," Quincee said. "I'll—"

"Never mind, Gene," the judge said. "I have a hacksaw. I'll see to it later for Miss Davis."

Quincee shot a quizzical gaze toward the judge. Why was he so nice all of a sudden? Why would he offer to help her?

"Uh-oh. I just remembered the roast I have in the

oven," Bette said in a sudden flurry. "Let me know if you need us to help you with anything in that pile of junk, my dear," she said to Quincee. She smiled at the children, who had drifted away to run about the yard, before saying, "Coming, Gene?"

"Be right there, Bette, love." Gene turned to the judge. "Say, Hamilton, did your grandfather ever find those old snapshots he promised to go through? Was a bunch from years back when our sons were just little tykes."

"I don't know that he ever did, Gene. There's a dozen boxes of old stuff he had in the attic that you're welcome to look through if you'd like."

"Now, Hamilton," Bette protested with humor as she edged toward the street. The others followed. "Don't get Gene started on your old stuff. We have enough of our own that we need to do something with. We're all getting too old to hang on to these leftovers, and our children don't want any of it."

"Why don't you have a garage sale?" Quincee threw the idea into the pot, strolling along.

"Thought about it," Mr. Bader said. "Daughter-in-law's got her eye on my coin collection, but she don't want nothing else of mine."

"A yard sale has come to mind," Bette said, seeming to forget her urgency to tend to dinner. "But Gene doesn't want to mess with one."

"Too much work," Gene said. "And too many people pawing through things, making a wreck of it."

"If it's done well, that can be directed and controlled," Quincee suggested.

"How do you mean?" Bette asked.

"You could combine your sales and efforts into one location. Have a neighborhood block sale. They're always popular. And if you combine your forces, there would be several of you on hand to help people with purchases while one person takes the money. That would give you more control."

Quincee stopped near the sidewalk. Dandelions sprouted around her ankles in all their golden beauty. Almost marking the property line, healthy grass from the judge's yard warred with her spotty weeds.

"I don't like the idea," the judge said. "It would disturb the neighborhood."

"Combining efforts into a group sale sounds wonderful to me," Bette said. "But, oh my, that takes a lot of work to organize such an event. I'm not sure I'm up to it."

"I could do it," Quincee said. She'd never handled one before, but she'd headed the committee for the school fair last year. "I'm very good at organization."

Hamilton gave her a pointed stare. She bit her lip and tried to ignore him. Why was he so skeptical? She *was* an organized person.

"Oh, but my dear," Bette protested. "You've just moved in here, and have so much of your own work to take care of."

"That's for sure," she replied. "But the kids and I have the whole summer to see to our own things.

And I can organize the sale and still paint my house this month.''

Providing her one credit card would stretch to cover the paint and supplies. And there was always the hope she might sell some things in the sale herself. A few dollars extra this month could be a lifesaver. Her enthusiasm for the sale suddenly became personal.

I can do all things through Him Who gives me strength, she mentally quoted.

''It really isn't a good plan,'' Hamilton insisted. ''It would bring too many strangers around.''

''Say, young lady,'' Mr. Bader said. ''What would you charge to do a thing like that? Ten percent?''

''Randolf, you're behind the times.'' Gene crowed at scoring one on Bader. ''Nobody does anything for only ten percent anymore. It's fifteen now.''

''You're both wrong,'' Bette said. ''It's twenty percent or more in these things. Estate sales and all that.''

''More?'' Aghast, Mr. Bader shoved his hand over his bald head and scratched an ear.

''I'd be quite happy to settle for ten percent,'' Quincee interjected quickly. ''As a favor to the neighborhood.''

''I'm really not in favor of garage sales. They're a hazard on neighborhood streets and they leave a mess behind. Who will be in charge to see that it's all cleaned up afterward? And there's no way to know if you'll make any money from one by the time all expenses are in,'' Hamilton insisted. ''It may be better to simply pay someone to come and cart your unwanted goods away. That way you'd deal with a reputable flea market business, and all the risks are the dealer's.''

"But you'd make more money with a yard sale of your own," Quincee said. "And they can be fun. Bringing several families together on the block to work the day can be almost a party. Perhaps we could make a trade for my services?"

"Trade?" asked Mr. Bader. "Like how? Trade what?"

"Like bartering. I'll take care of this garage sale, the organization, the preparations and the cleanup, in exchange for something you can do for me. That way no money is exchanged."

"Say, that's a dandy idea," Mr. Bader exclaimed. "What will you take?"

Bette's face lit with interest. "Bartering?"

"Well, if we barter, my fee will increase to the equivalent of fifteen percent or…even trade. What do you do?" Quincee asked. "Or have that I may want?"

The old man looked at Kyle, then at Quincee. "Got some fishing poles I don't use much anymore. My grandchildren don't live close enough to use 'em, and their parents don't like fishing."

"That'll do for a start," Quincee said. "Anything else?"

"Got an old upright piano. Needs repair. Nobody plays it anymore."

"Now that's a thought to keep!" Quincee let her

smile spread with enthusiasm as her heart leaped. A piano!

"Your house is too tiny to hold a piano," Hamilton muttered. "You'd have to haul it, anyway."

Quincee ignored his frown and pronounced, "I'll find a way."

"Beverly Kinney, down on the corner, gives piano lessons," Bette said in thoughtful tones. "I'll bet she'd give the children lessons in exchange for coming into the sale."

"That's the spirit. It's easy to barter once you get the hang of it," Quincee said.

"Quincee, it's lovely having a young family across from us," Bette said. "You put new life on the street. I really have to go attend my roast now. But come along for coffee later this week, and we'll get started on this garage sale."

"I really wish you'd give more thought to this, folks." The judge's protest grew stronger.

"Not now, Hamilton, dear," Bette said as she hurried across the street. "Later."

Hamilton watched the neighbors stroll away with consternation written on his features. He turned to Quincee and grumbled, "I wish you hadn't done that."

"Done what? What have I done now?"

"Offered to organize a yard sale."

"Why not? It's a great idea."

"No. It isn't. It'll create a pain in the—"

"That's only your opinion, Hap." As a neighbor, that was all he was entitled to, an opinion. She sud-

denly gave him a sassy smile, feeling liberated from
the restraints that he seemed to have imposed on her,
when in reality only her driving had been restricted.

"Hap?"

"You."

He stiffened. "I prefer to be called by my given
name, please."

"Those are your given initials. HAP. Hap sure is
a sight easier to say than Hamilton Paxton. Surely
you don't expect to be called Judge all the time? By
the way, what does the A stand for?"

"Adam. That's beside the point, Miss Davis."

"It might as well be Quincee. We're not in the
courtroom now, Hap. Er, Hamilton."

"Would you please listen?" His exasperation was
growing like those dandelions, she mused. She almost chuckled aloud, only surprised he hadn't ordered her to immediately root them out because they
were spreading into his perfectly kept yard.

"This is a peaceful, quiet neighborhood. A yard
sale isn't what we're about," he continued, stepping
closer to stand face-to-face.

Quincee lost her amusement.

With no hedge between them and no mammoth
court furniture to set him apart, he towered over her
by a full head. She had to tip hers back to look into
his eyes. A tiny scar sat just beneath his left brow,
and she spotted a hint of silver threaded with the dark
hair at his temples. But more than anything, she
noted the animation leaping from those cool depths

of gray irises. It excited a tiny kick in response as she realized the vitality of the male she faced.

My, my, my... Where had the judge gone?

"Garage sales are a pure nuisance," he continued his argument. She hadn't heard much of what he'd said in the last five minutes, but she responded.

"You don't have to join us if you don't wish. No one is forcing you into it."

"I don't plan to."

"Fine." She took a deep breath, feeling as though she had to have a fresh one to clear her thinking. "But a garage sale will benefit the ones who want to do it. Actually, I think we can have a bit of fun with it as well as make a little money."

"These folks don't need the money," he argued hotly. "They'd be better off following my suggestion of having a reputable dealer come and take care of any items they no longer use. Or give it all to charity."

Quincee tipped her head and softened her tone. "Is that your problem, Hap? You're too used to being the center of attention and having your way on the bench that you can't stand the thought of your neighbors ignoring your suggestions?"

Hap stepped back as though she'd hit him. His features seemed to go bland while he retreated behind his cool gaze. "Don't be offensive, Miss Davis. You're way over the line."

"Sorry about that, Hap." She did feel sorry to have chased him back into his cold reserve. "But you're the only one yet who seems to dislike the prospect of a block yard sale. Get used to it. This event is going to happen. And I can use the work.''

''You'll have to pay taxes on your fee, you know.''

''Not if everything is simply an exchange of favors with no money exchanged. I love bartering. It has a set of rules all its own and it answers many problems. Why, we solved our little problem the other day when the children worked off their debt, didn't we? That's barter. A bargain for me, as well, Hap. You gave us those beautiful strawberries, which the children and I enjoyed very much. In turn, I shared my labor of making the pie. It's as simple as that.''

''Not quite, when taken to a larger scale,'' he insisted. ''Bartering still demands taxes be paid on the equivalent of what that service is worth.''

''Fine. I'll declare it and pay the taxes if I must,'' she said, fuming. ''But our society loves a bargain. And bartering is based on a long forgotten simpler exchange of goods and services, in my opinion. As I'm a schoolteacher, my salary has to be supplemented some way, and this works for me.'' She raised an expressive brow. ''Believe me, I'm willing to bargain for anything and everything I can.''

With that, she turned on her heel and marched toward her front door. Behind her, Hap remained silent. She guessed he wasn't used to losing the privilege of having the last word on anything. He wouldn't subject his dignity to calling out to her retreating back.

By the time she strolled through the door, her smile had stretched into a grin.

Chapter Three

~

"Another fine June morning," Quincee said to herself not long after dawn on Sunday. She quietly pulled on cut-off denims and a light blue T-shirt printed with her school logo, and headed for the kitchen. The kids weren't out of bed yet. She didn't see any rush to wake them.

She made a cup of instant coffee and took her mug out to the backyard, wishing she had a Sunday newspaper to read. Her folks always had a Sunday paper when she and Paula were growing up. They'd fight over who got the cartoons first while Mom read the ads and Dad read the front page. Later they'd go to church and then spend the afternoon with Mom's sister, Aunt Beth, or their grandparents.

That was long ago, she mused. Her parents had died young, leaving Paula and her to cling to each other, and Aunt Beth and her family had moved to

Colorado. Life had moved on. But Quincee recalled those days with fond nostalgia, and she intended to give Kyle and Kerri as much home life and stability as she could make for them.

Strolling over to the old wooden bench under a slender oak tree, she wondered if she'd gain a splinter if she sat on it. But it looked inviting, so she sank down and stretched out her bare legs.

She lifted her face to the sun. She felt lazy. It was a lovely way to start a Sunday morning, even without a Sunday paper. Sundays should always have a special identity, meaningful and different from other days, she decided.

She and the children would let any work on the house go for today. They'd find something new to do, something to take them out of the daily routine. Didn't the Bible say the seventh day should be a day of rest?

"That's it," she murmured. "We'll go to church. It's just what we need."

Although her faith in God had never waned, she'd been lax in finding a church home these last few years. She and Paula had been raised with church attendance as part of their weekly routine, Sunday mornings and Wednesday evenings in prayer service, and she suddenly realized how much she missed it. She certainly could benefit from hearing God's word spoken aloud, of singing her worship. What did the scripture say? *Forsake not the gathering together?*

She'd have to look up the exact Scripture, she supposed, but she understood the gist of it. It was past time to see that the children had biblical studies.

Quincee wiggled her toes in a clump of dandelions, thinking about it. Could she sneak the car out?

Nah...she'd better not try to defy her restriction. Surely she could find a church within walking distance.

Happy with her plan, Quincee sipped her coffee. Still lazily enjoying the early sun rays, she set her cup on the ground beside her, swung her feet up and leaned back on folded arms behind her head. Humming a tune, she stared at the sky for long moments, mentally going over her list of things to do for the coming week.

Meet with Bette again about the neighborhood yard sale—they'd already sketched out early plans. Call the newspapers about placing an ad. Make flyers to distribute. Talk to Mr. Bader to see if she could inspect the piano he offered her. And finish scraping and sanding her house.

She'd spent the majority of her week hand-scraping four layers of old paint from three sides of her house; she had only one side left to complete. Laura promised to run her to the hardware store to buy paint. She'd already done a preliminary pricing by phone and knew just where to shop for the best bargain.

"Quincee?" She heard Kyle from the open back door.

The boy was another early riser. She often thought of the first hour of the day as their time, since they frequently discussed things that he was interested in without Kerri's bid for her attention to interrupt them.

"Out here, Kyle."

In turning to sit up, something caused her to glance over at the house next door. A flutter at the corner of her eye brought her attention to a second-story window. A bare-chested man appeared between the lace curtains, hair tousled and leaning on strong arms against the windowsill. She saw his chest expand and contract. Hamilton Adam Paxton, the Third, liked to greet the morning by breathing deeply in an open window, did he? Who could've guessed he'd be a fitness freak?

Across the distance, he seemed to be watching her. How long had he been there? Flashing an emphatic grin, she gave a saucy wave.

He disappeared behind the curtains, and his window slammed closed. Quincee folded her mouth, smothering a chuckle. Obviously, he wasn't amused. Had she invaded his space? Had he lost his sense of privacy on this side of his house? Her house had been empty so long, he might think it.

Kyle came out carrying a glass of juice and perched on the bench beside her.

"Hi, tiger. It's a beautiful morning," she said. "How about if we begin our day with a nice walk after breakfast?"

Several hours later, the three of them approached a large stone church building that had been a part of Independence since 1872. She'd called to find out the times of worship and found a map to tell her just how far they'd have to walk. A mile and six-tenths sounded just about the right amount to enjoy, she told the children. By the time they arrived, they'd welcome a chance to sit quietly and listen to God's word.

Quincee smoothed a hand over her long blue print skirt and ran an inspecting gaze over Kyle's clean jeans and white open-neck dress shirt. His short hair lay close to his head, and his face appeared shiny clean.

Kerri looked fetching in the yellow sundress Quincee had hurriedly dug out from the bottom of a drawer for the child to wear. A simple white knit T-shirt under the printed straps dressed it up a bit.

Actually, the dress was too short for the child, but Quincee hadn't had time to buy any new clothes for the children.

Who was she kidding? She hadn't had any extra money to buy new clothes for any of them. Well, the old sewing machine would have to come out of storage, she decided. Attaching a ruffle onto the dress's hem would solve that problem, and she could do some other long-needed mending while she was at it.

They climbed the concrete steps to the huge open front doors.

An older man, graying and with a limp, greeted them at the door with a handshake for her and a word for the children. "Good morning there, folks. How are you this fine morning? Welcome to God's house, young man. And young missy. Nice of you to join us. Go right on in and find a place to sit. There's an empty spot about halfway down this morning."

Another greeter welcomed them inside the foyer and handed Quincee a program.

The church sanctuary, already about three-quarters full, was filling quickly. Quincee guided the children toward the center as directed. They slid into a pew. Surprisingly, Kerri was subdued enough to remain silent as she busily looked around her. Kyle asked whispered questions about who the people on the stage might be and excitedly pointed out that several had instruments. Were they going to play?

Before she could answer, a tap on her shoulder caused Quincee to glance backward. Bette and Gene Longacre sat just behind them.

"Why, hello there, Quincee," Bette greeted with a smiling welcome. "And Kyle and Kerri."

Gene nodded at the children, murmuring, "How spiffy you look this morning."

Quincee felt warmed and unexpectedly at home.

"So nice to have you here to worship with us this morning," Bette said. "Oh, Quincee. I have three other people who are eager to join the yard sale. One lives a block down, and she said she'd be glad to help set up such an event, and they all love your idea of barter. Can we get together tomorrow?"

Bette ended on a whisper as the musicians began the opening song.

"Oh, sure," Quincee returned, also whispering. "Certainly."

She then riveted her attention on the opening of the worship service, silently praying to have a listening heart.

They all rose to join the first lively song of joy and thanksgiving. The children, wide-eyed with curiosity, gazed around them when a family with several children squeezed into the pew on their other side. Kerri stretched to her toes trying to see the song leader.

The morning went quickly. Quincee, drawn into the sermon of God's redeeming love, of His promises, felt lifted and filled with more peace than she'd had in months. Since before her sister's illness, she thought. She hadn't realized how hungry she'd been to hear it again. Closing her eyes, she silently thanked God for leading her to this church this morning.

Just before the close of the service, the minister announced a need to see the deacons for a few moments immediately following the service. He dismissed the congregation with the admonition, "Go home, go forth and share God's love throughout the week, and love one another."

Quincee and the children joined the sudden crush in the aisle. People greeted each other, someone mentioning the Royals' latest baseball score, another replying. A child begged to go swimming as soon as they returned home. Behind her, Bette repeated her promise to call tomorrow. Looking over her shoulder, Quincee responded with a nod.

Someone pushed down the aisle against the tide, and Kerri suddenly called, "Hap. Hap, here we are."

Quincee's head snapped around. Almost face-to-face, Hamilton stared at her, his eyes darkening in mild shock. A fleeting image of his earlier appearance in his window crossed her mind. Something told her he was thinking of that same moment. Heat rose in her cheeks. She felt trapped in the eddy of flowing humanity, while hung up in his gaze.

He recovered more quickly than she and switched his attention to the children. Kerri had already grabbed his hand and looked at him adoringly. "I didn't know you were at church, Hap."

Hearing the nickname, a portly man glanced at them curiously as he came out of a pew nearby, his gaze finally leveling on Hamilton. His mouth curved in what Quincee could only call a smirk. "Five minutes, Judge," the man said, and shoved his way down the aisle.

Irritation flickered across Hamilton's face, but it was gone by the time he answered Kerri. "I didn't know you were here, either, Kerri. Did you and Kyle find new friends at Bible class?"

"We didn't go to Bible class," Kyle told him. "We just came to church."

"Come early enough for the children's Bible study next week, children. You'd like it." Then flashing Quincee a suspicious gaze, he asked, "How did you come today?"

"We walked," Kerri informed him with pride. "We walked a hundred blocks."

The crowd around them thinned. Hamilton glanced at the small knot of men gathering at the front, his expression indicating he was hoping for a quick exit. Quincee followed his gaze and noted the pastor watching them expectantly.

"Sorry, but I must go," he said. "Deacon's meeting. But if you wait around for about ten minutes, I'll drive you home."

Quincee dropped her gaze. Really? He was a deacon at this church? Oh, great! Why didn't that surprise her? Of all her luck, she'd found a church she liked on the first try, and the judge was a deacon there. Was this a conspiracy to keep her under his watchful eye or something?

"That's kind of you, but not this time, thank you." She took Kerri's hand. "Come on, kids. Let's be on our way."

"See you later, Hap," Kerri said, letting go her hold on the judge. A tiny dimple appeared beside her mouth, worthy of Shirley Temple. "Can we come over and help in your garden today?"

"Um, I suppose so." His lightning glance surveyed Quincee's face. "Sure," he said with more force. "I'll, um, probably be out this afternoon. Just wait, all right?"

They were halfway home when Hamilton's sleek, dark sedan rolled to a stop at the curb beside them. "Why didn't you wait? Get in, I'll take you the rest of the way home."

"Thank you, but we're fine." Quincee kept a firm hand on Kerri and continued walking. Kyle marched a few yards ahead, dragging a large stick he'd picked up along the way. He dodged to the right, bounding at an overhanging limb.

"Kyle," she protested.

Kyle pretended he didn't hear her. Instead, he grabbed hold and swung in a Tarzan leap, landing miraculously on both feet. Quincee let out a sigh.

"I can have you home in three minutes," Hap said. "It's already hot out here."

"No, thank you." She tried to avoid raising her nose into the air or sounding self-sacrificingly superior or anything, but she just thought he needn't have any further chances to oversee her life.

She didn't want to be owing him any favors, either. Not unless they had a firm understanding about a barter exchange. Beside, it didn't hurt for the judge to realize how doing without a car changed one's daily perspective. She only wished he could experience it firsthand rather than by observation. "We are enjoying the walk."

"Suit yourself." He pulled away, his expression set.

Now she'd really insulted him, Quincee supposed. She hadn't intended to offend him—well, only a little. But she had wanted to exert her independence.

Hamilton drove home determined he'd be wasting his time to offer any further assistance to that obstinate bit of fluff living next door. What in the world had he been thinking to even try? Hadn't his position taught him that doing the Good Samaritan routine was wasted on most people these days? But her stubborn little chin and huge blue eyes somehow stirred his emotions.

Careful, Hamilton! She's a single mother with no evidence of having more sense than God gave a goose. She'll suck you in with saucy smiles and empty promises if you're not prudent, and spit you out like an unwanted core.

He hadn't much patience with the women of his generation. Like his late grandfather, he thought too many were irresponsible and careless in the extreme, never far from disaster because they acted without much care for the future. His mother had been one of those flibbertigibbets. But in all honesty, he couldn't say much for his father, either.

Uncomfortable with where those thoughts always took him, Hamilton forced his hands to relax on the wheel.

Quincee Davis seemed to fit that box of foolish woman to perfection. How could she have moved into that shambles of a house next door expecting to raise two children there alone? With all the work it needed to make it truly livable? It could have been bulldozed to the ground for all he cared. The neighborhood would look much neater without it.

Furthermore, he'd noticed that the young woman expected to do everything herself. He didn't exactly approve of single women declaring they didn't need a man. He was old-fashioned, he supposed, but it took two people to make those children, and although he'd been raised by his grandfather alone, he really thought children should have two parents if at all possible. Where was the children's father, anyway?

Hamilton parked his car, pulling it into his detached oversize garage with its neat workbench in the rear. His grandfather's old dark blue sedan still occupied the second half. He supposed it was time to sell it. His granddad had been gone nearly two years.

He'd returned to this house after years in an inner city apartment with all the mixed emotions of any inheritance, he supposed. After the age of five, he'd been raised in this house. He missed his grandfather, and the longer he continued to live here, the more he felt it was his rightful place. He was a man born too late for his time, he supposed.

But what had he ever done to deserve Quincee Davis as a neighbor? He was still figuring that out. Her refusal of a ride wasn't the end of the world, but he couldn't help feeling ruffled over the woman's insistence of having the last word in their conversations. Each and every time.

Stubborn woman! She liked having her own way and she certainly learned her lessons the hard way.

Thinking about her made his shoulders twitch. Quincee was one sassy woman. Her strawberry hair fit her. In his opinion, she needed far more help than she'd admit. Yes, she certainly was obstinate enough to learn her lessons the hard way.

And he'd just let her, by gum. He just would. Whatever compassion he'd been tempted to feel on the children's behalf was best kept to his side of the hedge.

He'd find it convenient to work outdoors for a time this afternoon. The tykes weren't nearly as annoying as he'd first thought them. They only needed a firm hand, and for some reason they liked him. The legal work he'd brought home to study could wait until evening.

He shut his car door firmly, and then his garage, before unlocking the back door of his silent house. Only the muted sounds of a slight breeze welcomed him home.

Quincee, on her side of the hedge, filled her afternoon with sorting through the last of the summer clothes they'd hurriedly stuffed into chests when unpacking. She flattened and hauled the last cardboard boxes to the trash bin, then cast a half-envious gaze over the side yard. She hadn't been invited to join the garden party, but there was no reason she couldn't wander over to see how the three of them were doing, was there?

The judge's vegetable garden took up a huge section of his backyard opposite the property line they shared. She half crawled through the hedge opening the children used, and went to find them.

"Now see this?" Hamilton spoke as she came around the corner. Three rounded backs huddled over a row of leaf lettuce. "That pesky rabbit has eaten more than his share of my lettuce. So we'll just place this fence around the edges of the garden like this."

He picked up a section of meshed wire with long stake wires and pushed it into the soft earth.

"When will the lettuce be ready for people?" Kyle asked.

"Actually, this is the last of it for this year. I've had many salads from this crop already, so I'd be happy to share the rest. Would you like to have some?"

"I guess so," Kyle replied in a dubious tone.

"The last of these snap peas should be good, too. If we leave them any longer, they'll be tough. Why don't you fill that old bucket with them and take them home?"

"Peas? Ugh." Kyle let his opinion of that particular vegetable be known as he squinted at Hamilton.

"I like peas," Kerri declared.

Quincee caught her breath on a spurt of laughter. Kerri *hated* peas, but obviously Hap's approval meant a lot to her.

"That's good. I'll wager you'll like these, Kyle. They're fresh and they taste much better than when canned or even frozen."

The thought of fresh lettuce and peas made Quincee's mouth water, but she was proud of Kyle when he asked, "Did we earn it?"

"You bet. Hand weeding takes special care. You two are really getting the hang of it."

This was the first time Quincee had been to Hamilton's garden, and she cast an assessing study over the entire space. Its neat rows and healthy plants could grace the cover of any home and garden magazine. She'd like to meet that outrageously bold rabbit who dared invade Hamilton's territory. They just might become friends.

She cleared her throat to let them know she was there. "It's time the two of you thank Hamilton for allowing you to play on his side of the hedge. But you should come home now. Laura is coming to visit later."

"Are we cooking hamburgers?" Kerri asked. "Can Hap come, too?"

"Um, sure, why not?" Quincee tipped her head. "Want to join us for a cookout?"

He gave her a quick, impatient glance. "Thank you, but I have work I must get done. I'd better decline."

So were they even now, Quincee wondered?

"Suit yourself." She let a smile curve as she stalked toward her yard.

"By the way, Miss Davis," he called after her. "I didn't forget that I promised to take that lock off your garage. I'll take care of it later, just as soon as I put away my garden tools."

"Thanks, Hap. Whenever."

She felt his gaze boring into her back, right between her shoulder blades. She was about to turn the corner and disappear from his view when he muttered, "If you must, call me Hamilton."

"Sure, Hamilton," she replied under her breath.

Chapter Four

"**Y**ou mean you still don't know what's in that garage?" Laura asked, her jaw slack with amazement. Her brown-eyed gaze followed Hamilton's progress as he retreated to his own yard, leaving few words behind him. He'd come over long enough to remove the lock, then left immediately, politely refusing a glass of lemonade.

The sun hung low on the horizon, still hot but beginning to lose its heat. Quincee and Laura lounged on a patch quilt thrown under the tree, the remains of their cookout and tall glasses of iced lemonade neatly stacked on the wooden bench, while Kyle and Kerri played tag, running circles around the house.

A huge feeling of gratitude always filled Quincee for her friend's generosity. They'd been fellow teachers at school from the first day Quincee had arrived, nearly five years before. Laura, older by ten years and more experienced, had been her mentor. Hers had been the shoulder soggy from Quincee's tears when Paula died. Recently, Quincee had cheered the loudest when Laura became the principle in an Independence school. Laura had assured Quincee a teacher's position there, one of the reasons she'd been excited to find a house on this street.

"Nope," Quincee replied. "Had other things to do. Other priorities. We're going to tackle it first thing in the morning, though. Want to come by and help?"

"How can you wait that long? I'd be chomping to get to it." Laura lowered her voice, tipping her head toward where she could see Hamilton between the hedge gaps as he strode toward his house. "Whew! That's the judge, huh? And he's the one who jerked your license?"

"Yep. He's the one."

"Has he said anything, referred to it at all?"

"Not a word. Guess he leaves his work behind when he leaves the courthouse."

"Is he always that stuffy?"

"Always," Quincee continued, barely above a whisper. "Though sometimes, when he doesn't know anyone is looking, he can become quite human. I think he's rather lonely."

"Well, it seems to me he'll make a problematical neighbor. I wouldn't want to live next door to him."

Quincee grinned. "Weelll, actually...I think he's kinda cute, if you're into serious men. It's just so much fun to tease him. He fumes in an interesting manner. And strangely, the kids have really taken to him.''

"They need a father figure, I suppose."

"Mmm," Quincee agreed.

"But Quincee, you'd better watch it. One day your odd sense of humor will get you into trouble, for sure.'' Laura's gaze roamed over the big house looming over Quincee's tiny one. "But you know, I think you're right. He is cute in a brooding, Rochester kind of way. Are you sure you can handle him?"

"Not at all." Quincee let her tone grow serious. "I don't think anyone *handles* Hamilton Adam Paxton, Three. He's too upright, too ingrained in old-fashioned philosophies for me. Really, Laura, don't worry about me falling for Hamilton. At this point in my life, I'm only hoping to make friends."

But he still had the finest of masculine eyes, Quincee thought. Perhaps the finest in the county.

"If you say so," Laura said, her tone dry. "Now we still have a couple of hours left of daylight. Are you really going to wait till tomorrow to see what's in that garage?"

"Nah. Let's have at it!" Quincee couldn't keep her irrepressible eagerness hidden a moment longer. "But I think we'd better wear gloves. Wait a moment and I'll find some."

She could find only one pair, though, and she offered these to Laura.

"Hap has gloves," Kerri said.

"Yeah, he wears 'em all the time when he works outside," Kyle added.

"I'll go ask if we can use 'em," Kerri said.

"No, don't, Kerri," Quincee commanded. "Don't bother him again. We've pestered him enough for one day. But do put on shoes, please." The children had run through the hose sprinkler to cool off and were still barefoot. "No telling what creepy crawlers we'll find in there."

"Ready, set, go!" Kyle called when they all were in place.

They made a great production of sliding back the old doors, one adult and one child wielding a door together. The huge panels creaked and groaned, bucking stubbornly along the rusted track until at last they stood wide. Stale air and shock waves of heat rushed out, making Quincee blink and Kerri cough.

Daylight reached only the middle of the structure, leaving the back corners in deep shadow.

True to Bette and Gene's declaration, stacks of cardboard boxes filled half the space nearly to the ceiling on one side. What looked to be a number of old bicycles in various states of wholeness and parts hung from wall hooks. Bundles of newspapers, yellowed and brown, a couple of barrel crates holding unknown items, worn-out tires and several pieces of outdated furniture haphazardly occupied a near corner.

The four of them stood in wonder for long moments. "And this is only what we see without stirring a finger," Laura muttered in awe.

"Bicycles," Kyle squealed.

"Looks like your luck is in, sport," Laura said, shaking her head in disbelief. "Yours, too, Kerri bear. But it may take a day or two to find one that's all together and still works. What say you, Quincee? Is there treasure enough here for you?"

"I scarcely believe it! Would you look at that?"

"What?"

"That rocker." Quincee moved forward and tentatively removed a box from atop a rattan rocking chair. She touched it to set it in motion, but too many other items jammed its path. She shoved at a tall piece of furniture, covered with torn freighting blankets. It proved to be too heavy and wouldn't budge.

"And there." She turned as something else caught her gaze. "Look at this old Formica kitchen table. What's wrong with it?"

"It's way out of style?" Laura suggested dryly. "And it has one leg short. See?" She pointed to a block of wood under one leg.

"Yeah, but it might be just the thing for Kerri and Kyle's art projects."

Quincee touched a small wooden table piled on top. "This is an antique, I'm sure of it. Its top is scratched and chipped, but it can be refinished. Why is this stuff even out here to gather mold and rot?"

"Well, it hasn't, as far as I can see." Laura cast her gaze toward the ceiling, looking for roof leaks. There didn't seem to be any. "This old garage has kept everything pretty dry, in spite of neglect. Lots of spider webs, though. Betcha you find mice, too."

"Uh-huh. Counted on the mice. Wonder what's—" Quincee heard shattering glass, and then an instant quarrel.

"Kerri!" Kyle protested.

"I was only looking."

"You shouldn'ta touched it."

"I didn't drop it. It just fell."

"Yeah, after you were messing 'round with it."

Quincee rounded the mountain of boxes. Kerri stood on top of a teetering chair with a ripped seat; its chrome frame declared it a match to the old kitchen table. Hanging from a nail above her dangled a pair of old shoe roller skates with wooden wheels, leftovers from two generations ago. Beside the chair, Kyle had been investigating the contents of a workbench.

"What broke? Did either of you get cut?"

"It was a jar with nails and pennies in it," Kerri explained.

"Pennies?" Quincee glanced at the concrete floor. True enough, pennies and small nails lay scattered everywhere. Many were rusty and bent.

"Well, I found it first," Kyle declared.

"Uh-uh. You were looking in that tin box with the baseball cards."

"Well, you said you wanted those ol' skates," Kyle replied.

"Never mind," Quincee said firmly. "We'll decide what you each can have tomorrow. Meanwhile, the two of you can pick up all the pennies and nails and divide the money between you."

"I really have to be going," Laura said, moving away from the heap of boxes. "It's been fun, kids. Looks like you have a day cut out for you tomorrow."

The children muttered goodbye, already bent to finding all the pennies they could.

"Closer to two or three days, I'm thinking," Quincee replied happily. "I'm sure we can sell half this stuff in the yard sale we're planning. Hopefully, I'll have enough money from it to buy paint outright instead of maxing out my last charge card."

As Laura drove away, Quincee began cleaning up the supper clutter from the backyard. That done, she listened to the kids count pennies on the back step as she put away chips and gathered the flatware to wash. She ran hot water into the sink, added a squirt of dish soap.

Pristine white. That was the color she wanted to paint the house. White, with jade-green shutters, she thought dreamily. Or perhaps a midnight blue for the shutters. Her little house would shine like a small jewel among the larger homes along the block and take its share of pride by the time she was finished with it.

Hamilton switched off his computer and leaned back in his chair. On his desk, he flipped open a manila folder and shuffled though several papers, reading bits of fact before making his own notations.

A Louis Armstrong jazz record played low from the shelved stereo in what was once his grandfather's study. His own, now, Hamilton felt, although he welcomed his memories of the long hours his granddad spent there. He supposed he should update his music technology as he had his computer system, but the old music bought him peace and a sense of family closeness.

He'd loved his grandfather deeply. He'd respected him even more.

He recalled the first time he'd entered this room. He'd been five, almost six, meeting his grandfather for the first time. His mother, Cecee Sand, didn't bother to hide the fact she hadn't wanted him any longer. But then, neither had his father, Richard, left behind in a California commune.

He'd stood straight, returning the old man's stare with silent defiance, while inside he'd screamed, "You don't have to want me...love me...nobody has to love me. I'll go back to the commune and live there on my own... I can take care of myself in the mountains...."

He hadn't known then that the California community, with its ideas of "liberated love, easy drugs and booze and living free" had already disbanded. His parents had come together in a more or less couple bonding, producing him without thought of marriage or any other real commitment. When they'd gone their separate ways, his mother eventually drifted back to the Midwest, taking him with her. Then came the time when he became a burden, and she'd left him with his father's father, Hamilton Adam Paxton II.

Going from life with his mother to life with his granddad had been a huge shock. Regular meals and a bed to call his very own had been the most pleasant.

His grandfather legally adopted and renamed him from Desert Sand to Hamilton Adam Paxton III. He'd tutored and fed him, body, mind and spirit, with a devotion the boy hadn't before encountered.

As he grew older in his grandfather's house, he'd soaked up the old man's fierce love and staunchly strict adherence to a biblical code as his lifeline. He'd also understood his granddad's deep hurt over his only son Richard's defection to the late sixties-early seventies rebellious culture.

Hamilton regretted the fact Richard had never made an attempt to reconcile with Grandfather. But his regret was for the old man. Only on rare occasions did he ever wonder where Richard was now. Richard knew where to find him.

As for his mother, Cecee had eventually married and settled in Georgia, producing three more children. He assumed she was happy. He'd seen her only a few times after she left him in Missouri.

He had recovered from those hurts long ago, but the circumstances of his birth and his early childhood had left him with deep-seated prejudice against irresponsible single parenthood.

A jamming of his doorbell sent chimes ringing softly throughout the house. He glanced at the clock with a frown. Almost midnight. Who in this quiet neighborhood would come calling at this hour unless there was an emergency?

He shoved back his chair and strode through the house to the front hall. Before he could reach the door, someone began to pound it.

Switching on the porch light, he looked out of his side window, spotting a small woman's figure. Beneath the soft glow, her face had little color.

"Quincee?" He swung the door wide. "What is it? It's nearly midnight."

"I saw your light." Her wide eyes shone with worry.

"Yes, I was just going up to bed. What's the matter?"

"I need your permission to drive my car. You can fix it, can't you? I have to have it."

He stiffened. One hint of fixing it made him seethe with anger. Only once or twice had anyone ever dared approach him about mending a ticket or giving a court-ordered release under the table. The results had been the hot side of his temper. His colleagues were eager to serve their profession with honor, but even among them, he enjoyed a reputation above reproach.

Yet something in Quincee's manner softened his reaction long enough for the next question. "Why, what's so desperate?"

"It's Kerri. She's running a high fever. I have to make a drugstore run to get something for it."

"A fever? How high?"

Quincee glanced over her shoulder toward her

house. Her face looked pinched and young. "One-oh-four."

"Where is she?"

"In bed." She turned and leaped down his front steps. She'd left her front door wide open. Kyle stood beside it, staring their way. Why would the boy be up?

He made a snap decision.

"Wait. I think a hospital emergency room is a better choice. I'll drive you. Get Kerri and Kyle ready to go while I get the car."

"Hap, I can't ask you—"

"You didn't. Now move!"

Quincee didn't argue. She raced across the front yards and spoke to Kyle. Hap shut his front door, grabbed his wallet and car keys and locked his house. He wasted no time in pulling his car out of his drive and into hers.

Quincee almost staggered under the weight of the child as she came down her two front steps. Quincee had covered Kerri in a sheet against the night air, and edges of it dangled at Quincee's knees. Kerri's head lolled in Quincee's shoulder.

Hamilton slid from the car, taking long strides to reach for Kerri. He held her while Quincee seated herself in the passenger seat. The child's fever burned his skin through the sheet.

"Get in the back, Kyle," he instructed.

Wordless, Kyle, shoes in one hand, wrenched open the back car door and scrambled in.

Hamilton started to lower Kerri in beside her

brother, but she whimpered. "Want Quincee," she said through a strangled throat. She started to cry, the sound feeble and hurting.

"Let me hold her," Quincee said.

"The seat belt…"

"I'll hold her firmly," she insisted. "Let me have her."

Hamilton bent and carefully placed Kerri in Quincee's lap, then worked to lengthen the seat belt. It wouldn't stretch to the lock over the two of them, and he gave up. Quincee soothed the little girl with cooing sounds while brushing her hair from her eyes.

"Sit tight," he said. "We're not going far."

As soon as he pulled into the main street three blocks from the house, he picked up his mobile phone and punched in nine-one-one. He asked to be connected to the emergency room desk at the hospital, and when he was, he asked to speak to the person in charge.

"With whom am I speaking? Belinda. This is Judge Hamilton Paxton speaking. Who's on staff tonight? Uh-huh. Well, how deep is your waiting room? Mmm…"

Hamilton drove unerringly with one hand while clutching the phone between his ear and shoulder, taking note of the traffic as they came to a cross street.

Quincee glanced at him over Kerri's head, her heart in her eyes. He had no time to explain.

"Is Dr. Terrence anywhere about tonight by any chance? No? Is either Dr. Levin or Dr. Toby on call?

Yes? Okay. Please call him and tell him I'm bringing
in a child that needs his immediate attention. I'd appreciate it if he could see her right away. We'll be
there in three minutes.''

"You know someone on the hospital staff?"
Quincee asked in awe.

"I've had occasion to mix and mingle," he explained. He didn't mind asking for this kind of favor
after all the support he'd shown the medical community over the years. Granddad had been on the
hospital board of directors. But he had no intention
of telling Quincee all that. "Here we are. Now sit
tight till I come around. I'll carry her."

He parked in the emergency drive, then came
around to scoop Kerri out of Quincee's lap. "Got
your shoes on, Kyle?"

"Yes, sir," Kyle answered. The boy's face looked
as stretched as Quincee's.

They hurried into the hospital. Quincee took one
look at the emergency waiting room, with nearly a
dozen people waiting for their turn to be seen, and
turned to Hamilton.

"Maybe we should try an all-night clinic?"

"No, this will be all right."

"But it will take hours for us to see a doctor."

"Dr. Levin doesn't live far. He'll be along shortly,
I'm sure."

A stocky man rose from his seat and nodded for
Quincee to take it. She murmured her thanks and
sank into it, holding out her arms for Kerri. Hamilton
placed Kerri on her lap, then told her he'd return as

soon as he'd parked the car. He strode out, hoping to heaven Dr. Levin was on his way.

Moments later, he strode down the short hall to the emergency waiting room. The three of them, Quince, Kyle and Kerri, huddled together like little lost lambs.

Quincee held the little girl close, letting her cheek rest atop Kerri's head. She crooned under her breath; Kerri slept, her body limp in Quincee's arms. Kyle perched on the edge of a chair beside her, minus his usual chatter, but as Hamilton came to them, he glanced up with great, unanswerable questions looming in his eyes.

Hamilton leaned against the wall beside them. He listened to the casual quiet murmurs around them and heard a nurse call the next name on her list. A couple rose, the man limping with a bandaged foot to follow where the nurse led.

Glancing down, he noted Kyle's white-knuckled clutch on the edge of the sheet covering his sister. The boy raised his lashes on welling tears, seeking his gaze. "Hap...is Kerri going to die?"

Chapter Five

"**W**hy, no, Kyle," Hamilton replied, careful to keep his tone even and assuring. "Kerri isn't going to die. Why would you think so?"

Hamilton met Kyle's gaze steadily, although he wanted to cast a swift glance at Quincee. The boy's fear leaped out of the small body to wrap tentacles of compassion around his heart. Why should the child be so afraid?

There was more than the usual casual concern going on in the boy's mind, he thought. He searched for words of comfort.

"Listen, Kyle. Kerri is sick, and a high fever sometimes scares us, but the doctor will see her very soon now. He'll give her some medicine to make her well. I'm sure she'll feel much better by tomorrow."

He glanced at Quincee. She bit her bottom lip, glimmers of moisture at the edges of her eyes. More than casual worry there, too. She shifted Kerri enough to free one hand, then patted Kyle's knee. "It's going to be all right, honey. I promise."

"Judge Paxton?" A male nurse called his name. "Dr. Levin is pulling into the parking lot now. We'll have to put you in day surgery, all our regular emergency examining rooms are occupied. Come along, I'll show you where."

Quincee struggled to rise with Kerri, her purse bumping her knee.

"Want me to take her?" Hamilton asked.

Quincee's arms tightened protectively around the child in an instant of panic before she shook her head. Panic? Where had that come from? Had something in his manner caused her discomfort?

He nodded, then slid his hand under her elbow, helping her rise with Kerri's weight. As they walked down the hall, the nurse, his name badge reading Mark, asked, "Did the admitting desk take all your medical information? Insurance?"

"Haven't had time for that yet," Hamilton answered. "We'll have to take care of the insurance forms on the way out."

"No," Quincee said quickly. Her glance bounced off his, her lashes dropping to cover the concern he caught there. "Ah...my insurance doesn't cover the children. I'll have to pay with a credit card. That will be all right, won't it?"

After a swift look Hamilton's way, the young man replied, "Sure, that'll be okay. But we do need to fill out this paperwork."

They reached the outpatient surgery department, silent and dark. The nurse snapped on lights in the large room, curtained into cubicles; his gaze raked it, checking the accommodations. He directed them to the nearest bed, made sure it had a clean sheet, then handed Quincee a clipboard with two forms on it. She clasped the clipboard awkwardly, dangling it away from Kerri's body.

"The doc will be here shortly," Mark said in parting.

"Here, let me take that," Hamilton said. He removed the clipboard from her hand.

Kerri stirred, crying when Quincee started to lay her on the bed.

"It's all right, honey bear," she soothed, stroking Kerri's arm. "I'm right here. I won't leave, and the doctor's coming. You'll feel better soon."

"It's gonna be okay, Kerri," Kyle said, leaning closer to pat his sister's arm. "Hap says so. We won't let ya die."

Hamilton was used to carrying responsibility. Even big ones. But the boy's confidence in his word struck him as a mighty obligation, one even bigger than his place on the bench required. It sent an unusual humbling arrow straight through him.

Still, he did wonder about Kyle's weighty concern. The boy was very young to even think about death, much less understand it. Yet at a much earlier age, he had worried about all sorts of basic life struggles. Like who would feed him his next meal, or where he'd sleep. True reality sometimes robbed a child of innocence, he well knew.

To help deflect Kyle's anxiety, Hamilton directed the boy to bring some chairs. "See, there's two right there beside that desk. You bring them over here so your mom can sit down. I'll bring this other chair, from beside that far bed."

In the nature of boys, Kyle scooted a chair into a screeching journey. He left it beside the gurney then went after another. Hamilton lifted one chair quietly and placed it closer beside the bed, and then gently pressed Quincee into it. She sank down, never letting go of Kerri's hand.

"All right, Kyle. Let's fill out what we can, here." Hamilton sat and leaned closer to the boy as he pulled a pen from his shirt pocket. "Okay…how does Kerri spell her name?"

"K-e-r-r-i L-e-a S-t-i-l-l-m-a-n," Kyle replied, spelling.

"Kerri Lea…your last name is Stillman? Not Davis?"

"Uh-uh. Davis is Quincee's name."

"Ah…yes. Okay." He pursed his mouth; he held his grandfather's old-fashioned views on such matters. He thought it troublesome for children to have different names than a parent. But it wasn't always possible and it had become a part of the modern world regardless of his views. Besides, it wasn't any of his business. "Now I know Kerri is five. When's her birthday?"

"I forgot." Kyle brushed his hair from his eyes,

streaks of blond gleaming in the overhead light. "It's in the spring."

"March twenty-fifth." Quincee supplied the answer.

"I know the address." Hamilton wrote a few minutes, filling in all the blanks he could. "Any allergies?"

Quincee shook her head.

"Who is her primary physician?" He paused, the pen an inch from the form. When an immediate answer wasn't forthcoming, he glanced up.

"Um...we haven't had one steadily," Quincee answered with a slight flush. "The clinic my sister used, ah, the one we've used when we needed one, is in south Kansas City, close to where we used to live. I suppose I could—should, rather—establish the children with a pediatrician in Independence. Especially before I register them in the Independence school system. Yes—" she blinked as though switching her thoughts took great effort "—it'll have to go at the top of our list of things to do. I should have thought of that before."

Hamilton returned his attention to the form in front of him. Just like a flibbertigibbet to wait to the last minute to take care of these things. Imagine! "And have they had the usual immunization shots?"

"Oh, I'm sure they have."

She didn't sound all that sure. Didn't she know? Again, the ballpoint hovered an inch above the clipboard. This time he didn't raise his gaze.

"Yes, of course," she added hastily.

Without looking up again, he made check marks, then ran the pen point down the sheet. "I guess that's all I can fill out for you, Quincee. I'm surprised..."

"About what?"

"I'd think you'd carry insurance coverage."

"I can't just yet. It's on my list of things to take care of just as soon as I can, but...the children weren't, ah, really eligible to come under my policy until...recently."

He raised a brow. Hesitant wasn't the usual quality that came to mind when he thought of Quincee. "I don't understand."

Before she could answer, the door swung open and the doctor came through. A comfortable-looking man in his early forties, Dr. Shawn Levin pushed his glasses more firmly on his nose as he greeted Hamilton with a friendly mutter and a you-owe-me gleam in his eyes. In very short order, he'd asked Hamilton and Kyle to wait outside and turned his attention to Kerri and Quincee.

Hamilton guided Kyle out the door, and they paused in the dim hallway.

"Do you want to return to the waiting area?" he asked the boy.

"No."

"Would you like a soda? I'm sure there's a vending machine around."

"No, that's all right." Kyle glanced at him, then slid to the floor, leaning against the wall, so close to the door that someone exiting could easily step on him. He curled his slight body around his bent knees and rested his chin there. His face remained pale.

An air of too much maturity settled about the boy, a feeling that said he'd set himself for a long wait, Hamilton thought. As though he'd done this before. Hamilton rested an arm against the wall above his head and crossed an ankle over his other foot.

"Kyle, why did you think Kerri would die?" he asked softly. "Has she been sick often?"

The boy barely glanced at him. "Not Kerri."

"Who, then?"

"Mom."

"Your mom's been sick?"

"Yeah. She was sick a long time."

"I'm very sorry to hear that. I wouldn't have guessed it. Quincee looks very healthy now."

"Not Quincee," Kyle corrected him. "Mom."

Hamilton felt his thoughts jerk off their track. He waited a moment until this new knowledge could settle. He cleared his throat before asking, "Kyle, what is your mother's full name?"

"Paula. Paula Stillman."

"Then who is Quincee?"

"Our aunt. She's my mom's sister."

At once, several facts scrambled to fall into a new pattern, creating a very different picture of his neighbors than he'd heretofore entertained. Kyle had used the past tense in referring to his mother. Did that explain the boy's deep fear that death was waiting for his sister? When had he lost his mother? How long ago?

He'd ask Quincee about that later in private.

All this did give him a different concept of Quincee, one less comfortable to live with. She wasn't quite the bit of fluff he'd thought her, he supposed.

She wasn't a single mother, either, but she was a single substitute parent. A brand-new one, he guessed. At least her heart was in the right place, her sense of duty. Her struggles to make a home for the children were certainly commendable. But he wasn't quite ready to let go of his notion that, normally, she was just a bit too brash for her own good.

"Where's your dad?" That was his next question.

"Don't know. Mom didn't, either. He travels, see. He loves us, but he just can't be around to take care of us much. Mom always said not to worry about it because we had enough love from her and Quincee to fill a canyon."

"I see." A wild and maverick streak of envy struck Hamilton, something he thought he'd packed away long ago. A mother who had loved her son with enough emotion to fill a canyon? Where did one find such creatures?

He yanked his irregular thoughts in with all the force of a cop with a restraint order. He had no room in his life for leftover envy. He knew for a fact such an emotion could smother him. He was better off not wanting something that wasn't meant for him.

The door beside them opened, and Dr. Levin came out, pulling his stethoscope from around his neck. "Okay, Hamilton. You did a smart thing, bringing in the youngster without waiting. It'll be a couple of days wait for the lab report to be positive, but I'm sure it's strep. I'm going ahead with an antibiotic. But strep is contagious. I'd like to see this young man's throat before we wrap up this visit.''

Kyle rose slowly, edging closer to Hamilton.

''It's all right, Kyle.'' He placed a hand on the boy's shoulder. ''There's nothing to be afraid of.''

Kyle's look told him he wasn't too certain of that; his feet dragged as he reluctantly followed the doctor into the room.

Through the open door, Hamilton saw Quincee pulling the sheet around Kerri once more, Kerri's head resting on her shoulder. The child's eyes were lackluster, her cheeks still flushed. He stepped forward, shoving aside his feelings of intrusion. ''Let me take her now. You'll need to stay with Kyle. I'll be just outside.''

This time Quincee didn't protest. Kerri didn't seem to mind when he gently shifted her onto his shoulder. Her arm slid up trustingly to hook around his neck, her skin against his hot and baby soft. Kerri wasn't much past a baby, at that, he mused. Though he'd often observed families with small children, he'd never held a baby or small child before. For the first time ever, he wondered what it would be like to become a father.

The thought scared the stuffing out of him, and he blinked it away.

He walked the hall, searching for a bench or a waiting area, but strolled back when he found none. The door opened a moment later. Kyle jumped down from the examining table, eager in his relief that his exam was over.

Quincee came out, taking a deep breath, tired lines etching her eyes. She silently reached for Kerri. He was about to mention he'd bring the car to the front entrance when the doctor spoke.

"Okay, Hamilton. You're next."

"Me?" His head jerked around. "My throat isn't sore."

"Uh, yeah. But just in case, let me have a peek at the old throat," Shawn said. The corner of his mouth edged up, and Hamilton narrowed his eyes at his friend. He thought Shawn was altogether enjoying his position as the doctor in charge a little too much.

"You're kidding."

"Nope. Kyle tells me he and his sister have been helping you a lot in your garden," Shawn continued. "You've been in close proximity with the kids."

"But, Shawn, I've had my tonsils removed. I never get sick. Besides, isn't strep usually rampant in the winter?"

"Strep doesn't always need tonsils to set up a flare. You want to stay well, don't you?"

"It's okay, Hap," Kyle said, slipping his hand into Hamilton's palm. "I'll stay with you while he looks down your throat. It feels yucky, but it doesn't really hurt."

The boy's blue gaze coaxed with a trust so innocent, Hamilton felt his heart do another tumble and stretch.

He shifted his gaze to Quincee.

"Don't look at me," she said, raising her brows beneath tumbling red-blond curls, her eyes gleaming in sudden amusement. "Dr. Levin has already taken a culture sample from my throat. I never get sick, either. But strep..." She shrugged. "I'd hate to pass it along."

The untamed thought of being that close, close enough to that tempting mouth to pass along an infection sent his imagination spiraling. And then it hit him. He hadn't realized he found Quincee... tempting.

What on God's green earth was wrong with him tonight?

He abruptly turned and marched himself into the examining room. Twenty minutes later, they left the emergency room behind and made a stop by the all-night pharmacy before heading home. He and Quincee were almost silent as they traveled. In the back seat, Kyle had fallen asleep.

Hamilton carried the little girl into the house, laying her down in the tumbled double bed to which Quincee directed, while Kyle stumbled into his own bed in the next room. It took Hamilton only a moment to realize Quincee and Kerri shared the room. Sparsely decorated, he wondered how long Quincee thought she could live this way. He knew this house, knew it hosted only the two bedrooms.

Quincee leaned over the bed, straightening Kerri's slender little arms and legs with a depth of sweet woman's tenderness that got right to him. He'd seldom viewed such honest emotion. A raw wanting ran over him like water from a shower. How could he, at his age? Sweet Lord in heaven, he was nearly thirty-three years old—a bit overgrown, one would think, to still want something so childish.

Mentally shaking himself, he rushed for the front door. He had to get out of there. Now. He was regressing to a sniveling fool. The child had received the medication she needed, and Quincee... He wasn't required anymore.

"Hamilton." Quincee halted him as he reached the door. He half turned, not wanting to look at her again, needing to run back to his own quiet, perfectly ordered, *lonely* house. There he wasn't reminded of what wasn't his.

Quincee stepped closer, laying a hand not much bigger than Kyle's on his arm. Nails short and clean, her fingers ringless, her thumb wrapped against the quickening pulse in his wrist. Just that one tiny area of skin on skin, bringing him warmth. He'd never imagined anything so...connected.

"Thank you." Her murmur was soft and low. "I don't know how I'd have gotten along without you tonight."

"Glad to help," he mumbled.

He stumbled out and was halfway across the lawn before he remembered his car. It still sat in her drive.

Chapter Six

Quincee kept to the house for the next several days while Kerri recuperated. She hauled her only television set into the bedroom and set it up so that Kerri could watch her favorite children's programs. She spent time telephoning for quotes on table rentals and newspaper ad space for the coming sale. Bette came over one morning and they made lists of people who wanted to participate in the sale.

Between times, Quincee read to Kerri from all the children's books in her stacked boxes and played board games and dominoes. She slept on the living room couch so the child could have the bed to herself.

It made Quincee wonder what she would do when school began again and she had to work full time with one of the children sick. What did her students' parents do? Her colleagues? Many had extended family to help out, or they traded with friends. Or they simply took personal leave from work when they had a sick child. But that couldn't be the solution every time, she knew. She'd have to investigate sick-care alternatives.

It was another item for her top priority list.

When Kerri began to feel better, Quincee dug out a slate and chalk, setting the child to practice her alphabet. Kerri knew how to print her name and Kyle's.

"Show me how to write your name, Quincee," Kerri begged. She picked up a pink chalk stick. "And Hap's."

"Uh, well, here's mine." Quincee printed carefully, hoping if she didn't respond to the second name Kerri would forget about Hamilton's.

No such easy luck.

"How do you spell Hap?"

Quincee hid her sigh, sat on the bed beside Kerri and spelled out Hamilton. "But I think he would prefer to be called Judge Paxton."

"Is that my Hap?" Kerri's blue eyes shone.

"Yes, that's him."

"But you call him Hap."

"Well…most of the neighbors call him Hamilton and I've begun to call him Hamilton, too."

"That's a funny name."

"It's a family name, I suspect." Quincee played with a blond strand of Kerri's hair, then reached for a brush. "But people wouldn't think it very respectful to call him Hap. Especially children."

"But I like Hap. He lets *me* call him that."

"Couldn't you sort of change your mind about that?"

"Uh-uh." Kerri shook her head emphatically.

The phone rang, and Quincee made a dive for it. At least she could put off the issue of what the children called their neighbor until another day.

"I think we'll have six people coming to tomorrow's evening meeting," Bette Longacre said when Quincee answered. "And two maybes. But we have a confirmed eight households along Clover Street who want to join the sale, and four on Washington."

"Great work, Bette. Now are we firm on our sale date? Ten days from now, the last weekend in June?"

"Yes, indeed. I wouldn't let that get away from us. I say we've got to strike while the iron is hot."

"Yes, ma'am." Quincee smiled into the phone, liking Bette's spirit. "All right, then I'm going to call this ad into the papers. It's already written."

Quincee and Bette chatted a few moments about other points of the sale, then ended the call.

Kyle grew restless, asking for the dozenth time that week, "Quincee, can I go and get those bikes down from the garage?"

"All right, Kyle, you little bulldog," she teased. "We'll do it today. I need to clean out more of that stuff, anyway, so I'll be in the garage, too. Have to see what we can sell for ourselves."

The sale couldn't come any too soon for Quincee. She'd maxed out her credit card with the hospital bill, and her cash was running dangerously low. She'd have to do a bit of creative stretching with the bills until her next paycheck.

It was a hot day, and without sufficient air-conditioning, the house was stuffy. The garage, with wide-open doors, surely would be cooler. She felt as eager to work out there as the boy.

"Right after lunch, okay? But you know we don't have much money to spend on just stuff this summer. I expect those old bikes need new tires, at the very least. Do you promise to be patient and not hound me while we save the money to get them repaired?"

"Uh-huh. I promise, Quincee. I just wanta see 'em. That's all. I'll be real good about waiting, I promise."

"Okay. You've been a good kid." She ruffled his hair, then leaned to hug him, knowing his needs had gotten shoved aside somewhat the last few days. "The best, in fact. So we'll put getting those bikes into shape on our second most important list."

As soon as lunch was cleared away, they headed outside.

"Now, Kerri," she instructed, setting the little girl on a blanket in the shade of the oak tree. "Be good for me one more day. You stay right here and play with your dolls, please, while I take the ladder out and get those bikes down. We'll have to see how much repair they need, but that's an excellent project for Kyle. Then I'm going to sort through some of the things in the garage. I'll be in plain sight so that you can call me if you need me. Okay?"

Kerri nodded. Quincee lugged out half a dozen each of pillows and stuffed animals, and Kerri seemed happy enough playing princess in the midst of them.

Mr. Bader drifted their way, chatting about nothing much, telling them stories of his youth, his children's lives, and about how the neighborhood used to be. "Lots of kids around then. After school, they'd swarm in the street to play football, baseball. Sometimes we could shoo them off to the park, but mostly, they liked to play in the street, or in that vacant lot at the far end of the block next to Lowrys."

He hung around long enough to give his opinion of the bicycles. "Need lots of sanding, gotta get that rust off. There's a bicycle shop in town, they do some trade in used bikes. They'll know what kind of tires you should buy."

About the partial set of plain pink dishes Quincee found wrapped in newspaper dated from 1972, he said, "We had some like those once, Denise and I. She thought they were out of style and wanted new ones. Now those sell for good money at the flea markets."

"Do you really think so?" Quincee asked, holding a plate up to the light as she studied it. There were no chips that she could see. "How much?"

"Oh, a few bucks, at least. Seems silly to me, them costing more now than they did when new. Say, if I can find what's left of my old set, d'you think I should put them in the yard sale?"

"Only if you want to sell them, Mr. Bader. But if

they really match these, then we might show them side by side. And remember, the dealers always come early, so it would be a good idea to shop around a day or two before our sale to see what the going rate for them may be."

"By gum, that's a good idea, Miz Quincee. I think I'll do that tomorrow. But I'm gonna look for my box of dishes tonight."

That's where Hamilton found them. He was home early; Quincee heard his garage door rumble open, then his car door close. Mr. Bader called to him, and Hamilton dropped his jacket onto his back porch steps and pushed past the hedges where the children always came through. The hole was widening with each use.

"Hap!" Kerri enthused, hopping up from her pile of pillows and bears. No doubt about it, no one could miss the adoration in the child's expression.

"Hello, there, Kerri. I see you're feeling much better today." Hamilton's voice held deep compassion, a tenderness for the child that Quincee had noted before. He had called each evening, asking how Kerri was feeling, but he hadn't lingered over conversation.

A little to her regret. She liked his deep voice and liked the adult conversation.

"Uh-huh. But I can't go anywhere yet," Kerri explained. "Quincee says she needs a sitter or an errand boy or a night run."

"An errand boy?" Hamilton stiffened, his gaze leaping toward Quincee, who was dangling over the edge of a barrel. She came up, another news-wrapped package in her hand, her gaze innocent. He narrowed his eyes at her. "A night run?"

"Oh, that's not what it sounds, Hamilton," Quincee said, flashing a grin. Must he question everything she did or said?

"Oh?"

"Not a bit. My friend Laura offered to run by the grocery store for me, but she has a date, so it will have to be after her movie or whatever."

She wore a lemon-yellow sun top, cut-off jeans and sandals today. His gaze seemed locked on her bare shoulders as though he were counting her freckles.

"Do you need groceries?" he asked.

"Could use a few things."

"Is that all?" Hamilton dropped his voice, moving closer while Randolf Bader was busy with Kyle's inspection of bicycle parts. His gray gaze pinned her as neatly as if he'd used a nail gun. "You weren't planning on using your car or anything?"

Quincee turned belligerent. After their shared worry and closeness over Kerri's illness, how could he backslide in his opinion of her?

"No, Judge Paxton. Not for another week, at least, is it?" She bit off another snappy comment that would refer to his causing her loss of driving privilege. "I can't leave Kerri, can I? I simply need someone to make a grocery run for me."

"Well, why didn't you say so, little lady?" Randolf Bader spoke, coming over to join them. "I used to go shopping for m'wife Denise once in a while. I c'n do it. In fact, there was a time when you'd have had several such offers from this neighborhood.'' He shook his head sadly. ''Not so easy, these days. Sometimes don't know who to trust.''

''That's very kind of you to offer, Mr. Bader. I may take you up on it.''

''Now you just let me know what you need, milk and bread and whatever.'' He stood a little straighter and smoothed the fringe of hair at the back of his head. ''I'd be glad to get it for you while I'm out tomorrow.''

Bette Longacre, gathering her mail from her box across the street, spotted them and sauntered over.

''How's little Kerri today? Out and about, I see.''

The grown-ups began to chat about the coming yard sale. Kyle wandered over to them, a comic book in hand.

''Quincee, can I have these?''

''Shh, just a minute, tiger,'' she whispered. ''The adults are talking.''

Quincee returned her attention to Bette's comments about who was offering what at their proposed sale. Kyle stood by patiently while he turned worn pages of a faded comic book.

''Wondered where you'd gone to, Bette,'' Gene Longacre muttered as he came across Quincee's yard. ''What's up?''

''Nothing to interest you much,'' Randolf said. ''The boy here is trying to get a working bike out of these old parts. Reckon he needs new tires, for one thing.''

''And the Sayers are putting up a sailboat,'' Bette said to Quincee. ''They've bought a new one, and don't want to haul this one down to the lake or a dealer. They think they can sell it just as easily in the block sale, anyway.''

''That's terrific,'' Quincee said, her enthusiasm high. ''That's one of the items we'll feature in our flyer advertisements. It will pull in a lot of buyers, I'm sure.''

''It'll draw a lot of idlers,'' Hamilton said, turning down his mouth. ''I hope all of you will be alert.''

''But many of these people will buy items from other tables, Hamilton,'' Quincee explained. ''Safety is an issue we should discuss at our meeting, though.''

''I'd recommend you have several people who are free to simply watch the crowd flow,'' Hamilton said.

He slid his subdued green tie from around his neck, rolled it into a ball and stuffed it into his pocket. Then he unbuttoned his shirt at the neck.

Quincee watched his long, masculine fingers make slow movements with fascination, recalling the tender way they had wrapped around her arm the other night. His help had seemed perfectly natural, his light touch that of a welcome friend. Why then did she suddenly feel warmer simply watching his hands?

''Now that's a thought,'' Randolf said, nodding.

"Hey, boy." Gene almost gurgled. "Where did you get your comic book?"

Kyle glanced up. "In one of those boxes."

"Are there more of 'em?"

"Yeah. A bunch."

"Oh, my goodness!"

Startled out of her concentrated conversation with Bette, Quincee looked around. So did the others.

"What's the matter? Is it, um, an undesirable subject?" Quincee reached for the magazine, looking at the masculine cartoon figure, cape flying, that graced the cover. "It seems just the usual adventure to me."

"Nope." Gene shook his head. "I mean it's an all-right comic, nothing the boy shouldn't be reading. I'm just pretty doggone sure it's a collectible, that's all."

"Let me see that," Randolf said. Quincee handed over the magazine. Randolf flipped through the pages a moment. "Y'know, Gene, you got something right this time. By gum, you sure do. I think this is worth real money."

Gene gave the other man a sour glare. "I just reckon so. I know what I'm talking about. I had some of these as a kid, myself. And my boy collected his share."

"Comic books are worth money?" Bette asked, incredulous.

"Actually, these collections are going for a tidy sum," Hamilton added, losing his aloofness. He stepped closer to look over Gene's shoulder. "Perhaps we'd better rescue Kyle's treasure and see what he's got.''

He rolled his sleeves to his elbows.

"Kyle, hon, show me which box you found these in,'' Quincee said.

They all trooped into the garage. Kyle led them toward the back, climbed on a wooden crate and pointed to a box on the back wall shelf. Hamilton hauled the heavy cardboard box down and found a gift box within. Inside the second box lay a stack of a dozen well-preserved comic books. He flipped through the one on top.

"Yes, I think you should have these evaluated by a reputable dealer, Quincee,'' he said, and handed her the box. "I wouldn't put them in the yard sale.''

"Hamilton's right, Quincee,'' Gene said. "Find out what these are worth from a dealer. There's one on the square who deals with old comic books.''

"Well, these are Kyle's,'' she said, looking at the boy. "He found them. What do you think, tiger? Do you want to see what they're worth?''

"Uh-huh,'' he said as he nodded. "Can we go see tomorrow?''

Quincee didn't bother to glance at Hamilton. She still had ten days left to serve without the use of her car, and there were other things that had to come first. "We'll go just as soon as we can, Kyle. But that may take a few days.''

"I'll take you,'' Hamilton declared, surprising himself. He'd surprised the neighbors, too, by the expressions on their faces.

"You will?" Kyle said, his face lighting up. "Tomorrow?"

"That's very kind of you, Hamilton," Quincee said, her chin thrust out in challenge. "But we couldn't impose on you any more than we already have."

Bette glanced from Hamilton to Quincee, a sudden knowing gleam in her eyes.

Hamilton checked his watch. "We can take a quick trip right now, if you want to, Kyle, and catch the shop before it closes for the day. How about it?"

"Sure. Can I, Quincee?"

"Really, Hamilton, you don't have to do this." Quincee's voice dropped a notch. "We shouldn't take more of your time."

"It's not a problem, Quincee," Hamilton insisted, his voice warm while he met her unspoken challenge. "I may have a favor to ask of you one day soon."

"Oh." Quincee blinked, unable to hide her surprise. Then her face brightened. "A barter? All right, what can I do for you in return?"

"Well, we'll leave you to it, then," Bette said, a small smile playing on her lips. She laid her hand on Gene's arm to urge him away.

"Might as well give me your grocery list," Hamilton said as Randolf followed.

"Only when you tell me what service I may do for you in return."

If he didn't know better, Hamilton mused, he'd take that as an...unethical offer. That girl better watch herself or she might someday just find herself in a bind she never intended.

Hiding his thoughts, he let a resigned expression flit across his face before he said, "All right. I need to have an electrician come in and do some rewiring of my house. I'd like someone to be there when the work is done, but my schedule doesn't permit time off until later in the summer."

"Great. I can do that. Let me know when you have your schedule in place."

Hamilton nodded. "Now, how about it? Kyle and I need to get going if we're to reach the bookstore before it closes for the day."

Quincee's smile took on a saucy tilt. "Sure, fellas. I'll see you both later. But Judge Paxton, I'll hold you to our bargain. A service for a service."

Hamilton let out a deep sigh. The woman was impossibly stubborn. But that smile got him right in the gut, and he didn't know what kind of armor to wear that would shield him from it.

Chapter Seven

 ~❦~

Hamilton let Quincee into his house early one morning the following week. Kerri and Kyle trailed her, their eyes big with wonder. Quincee tried to hide her keen interest, but she admitted she'd been enormously curious to see inside Hamilton's home.

As expected, the two front parlors and dining room were large and high-ceilinged. Decorative molding snugged against the ceilings in century-old splendor, and the front hall oak staircase curved upward with grace.

Quincee knew women who would mortgage a good right arm to own this Victorian beauty. It was a lot of house for a man alone.

The parlor furniture was rather shabby, in a traditional style but otherwise nothing special. It looked as though it hadn't been moved an inch from where it had originally been arranged for twenty years.

Hamilton needed to update more than the house's wiring, she thought.

Then it struck her. He didn't use those rooms. Everything appeared precise, and it hadn't been dusted in quite a while.

He led them toward the back of the house and into his library. Dark paneling and drapes made it dim, even though he switched on the overhead light. An old mahogany desk sat in one corner, its legs ornately carved, its surface piled high with folders and books. A computer unit, looking out of place in the room's atmosphere, occupied a spot nearby.

Her gaze swung to the opposite side of the room. Stacks of books lay on the wide oak flooring near the edge of the large rug, floor-to-ceiling bookcases overflowed with ancient volumes, and colorful travel, garden and news magazines tumbled over a basket, which lay on the floor by a chocolate-colored leather lounger. A dirty coffee cup sat on the small table by the matching sofa. Two brass floor lamps rose on slender stems to light either end.

Behind the seating, long double windows overlooked his side yard. The side that joined theirs. She wondered how much time he spent looking out.

This room was where he spent his time, Quincee realized. It shouted "masculine territory."

"Sorry about the dust and clutter," he muttered as though just noticing it. "I used to have someone come in to clean every week, but I lost her when she and her husband retired to Arizona. Haven't had time to get someone else."

"Never mind that," she replied, trying to keep a smile to herself. It amused her to find something very normally male and imperfect about the judge. Obviously, he hated to clean house.

"Yeah. Well, I've sketched out the rooms where I want additional outlets, but I'll show you, as well. The electrician said it might take more than one day if they run into trouble with the current wiring. Some of it needs replacing. Granddad had a new furnace and air-conditioning unit put in a few years back, and a new roof a couple of years ago. But he hadn't gotten around to doing a lot of improving except to the basic wiring. I took the liberty of scheduling for a second phone line to be put in, too."

"Whatever you need done, Hap, you have my day. Er, Hamilton."

As she corrected herself, Hamilton glanced up from his sketch pad and captured her gaze.

When his eyes went dark, Quincee caught her breath. She waited for him to toss a terse command to remember his name properly, but it didn't come. Instead a heightening awareness leaped out of those gray depths, sending all kinds of signals down her body. Signals that she'd ignored before now—or at least she'd pretended to ignore. But she faced up to them now. Those fizzy feelings that raced around her veins grew stronger each time she found herself in this man's company.

It reminded her that they were two very single, very healthy adults.

"All of it?" he murmured.

"All of…what?" She swallowed, her mind gone blank.

"Your day."

"Oh. Um, yes, of course."

"What's this?" Kyle asked from the corner opposite the desk. He spun a wheel from an outdated eight-millimeter movie projector he'd found.

Hamilton yanked his attention from Quincee and strolled over to where the children were exploring the objects on another bank of shelves. "It's an old movie projector that belonged to my grandfather. He loved taking home movies and left me quite a collection."

Those movies had taught him what little he'd really known of his father. Or at least of his father's boyhood. Richard Hamilton Paxton, better known as Pax among the California commune flower children he'd joined well over thirty years before. He'd never returned to Missouri.

It had broken Granddad's heart. Over the years, Hamilton and his granddad had both tried to keep track of Pax. On rare occasions they'd heard from him. But not often. The last time Hap had any communication at all was two years ago when Granddad died. Pax had sent him a note with simply "sorry" scribbled across it.

"Would you like to see some funny old cartoons with it?" he asked Kyle and Kerri, shoving away the empty emotions of desertion. He'd had Granddad. After his years in the courts, he knew many children had no one to care at all. But his hard-edged opinions toward people who blithely produced children with little thought for their ultimate welfare would never soften.

"Uh-huh. Where are they?" Kyle answered.

"These canisters are full of them. And of me and friends." His tone lightened while his fingers trailed down the stack of round metal canisters, naming them. "Summer camp when I was ten, learning archery. And eleven and twelve, swimming. Running track in high school. Neighbors and friends. But my granddad loved filming the goings-on at the square. Parades and Christmas. It was a much busier place when he was young than it is now. I think Granddad even has a shot of old Harry walking the square."

"Who's old Harry?" Kerri asked.

"He was a very important man who used to live in our town. Harry Truman was once our president. Have you never been to see his home?"

Both children shook their heads.

"Quincee should take you sometime. And to see the presidential library."

"Sometime I will," Quincee assured them.

"What about the cartoons?" Kerri asked.

"Sometime soon, we'll set it up."

"Cool." Kyle exclaimed. "When?"

"Well…"

"After the neighborhood sale, Kyle." Quincee spoke with firmness, bailing him out. "We'll be very busy until that's over. Now don't bug Hamilton about it, okay?''

"Aw…" Kyle made a face, then agreed reluctantly.

"I won't forget, Kyle," Hamilton promised. "We'll make time for it soon."

Hamilton dug out his extra front door key and gave it to Quincee. "Steve—the electrician—has your number and house address. He also knows you're going to oversee the work. He said they'd be here around midmorning."

"We'll take care of it," Quincee assured him. They all trooped out together.

As promised, Steve and his assistant arrived a few minutes after ten. She and the kids let them in and showed Steve the house sketch that marked where Hamilton wanted additional outlets.

After Steve turned off the power, it seemed a perfectly natural thing for her to do while he made his trips up and down the back staircase to the basement—Quincee dusted. Everywhere on the lower floor. She found the broom closet next to the basement stairs off the kitchen and hauled out the dust mop. Not finding anything to use for the furniture, she sent the children running home to get an old T-shirt from her pile of dust rags. "And bring that lemon furniture polish," she called after them. "And the vinegar."

The three of them cleaned out a spiderweb hiding

in the front parlor corner and then polished all the wood furniture before going on to the stair railings and treads around the centered carpet.

The ancient kitchen linoleum floor no longer held a shine, she later concluded after earnestly trying to give it one, but at least she could clean it. She'd found the countertops neatly arranged and with little clutter, but she took the opportunity to wipe them thoroughly.

After tuna and egg salad sandwiches for lunch, which Quincee had brought from home, Kerri curled up and napped in front of Hamilton's television in the library while Kyle stretched out on the floor and amused himself with a chess set.

Quincee tackled the lower floor windows. She had to use a small ladder to reach the areas high above her normal reach but was pleased with the results. But she came to the conclusion that every window treatment in the house needed replacing.

The judge had almost as much to do to update his home as she did hers.

About three, Steve left to pick up supplies he needed, promising to return within the hour. She folded herself on the floor beside the children, her back resting on the leather chair. She stared at the room, especially the drapes. How long had they been in place?

She couldn't stand it another minute. Rising, she fetched the small ladder again from the kitchen closet.

In the library, she carefully unhooked the dusty drapes, intending to give them a good shake outside. Dust flew everywhere, making her cough. She folded the heavy fabric at her feet.

Without the drapes, the room was flooded with afternoon sunshine. Dust danced in the light shafts, coating everything on Hamilton's desk, the one area that had appeared free of it.

"What are you doing?" It didn't surprise her at all to hear Hamilton's deep, cavernous voice halfway through her effort to reach the highest corners of the windows. It seemed destined for Hamilton to catch her in the worst possible moments.

Kerri popped up from her place in front of the television, coming forward to slip her hand in his. "Hap, can we go work in the garden? I'm tired of indoors."

"Me, too, Kerri. That's why I'm home early." He answered the child but then turned to Quincee.

"Exactly what it looks like," Quincee answered over her shoulder. "I'm cleaning these windows. They were long overdue."

"I realize that," Hamilton replied with only a hint of exasperation. Or he would have, had he given any thought to it. He didn't recall the last time they'd been cleaned.

His boyish self-concept and confidence had been built in this familiar room; the hours he'd spent here with Granddad were beyond count. It was comfortable with memories, but his honesty, as he glanced about him, compelled him to acknowledge how shabby it had become.

"And the drapes?"

"Actually, they need a good cleaning, but—"

"But what?"

"They're really old, Hamilton. I'm not sure they'd stand up to a cleaning. You should think about replacing them."

"I suppose you're right." He frowned, running a finger over his desk. Even this beloved old desk could use some refinishing attention. "Nothing's been changed in here since Granddad used to entertain his cronies every Thursday night. But I didn't expect you to clean my house, you know."

"We didn't mind, did we, kids?" She shrugged and released an impish smile. "We had to stick around anyway."

Just then, the power came on. They heard the rumble of the air-conditioning unit as it came to life.

Steve appeared a moment later, wiping his hands down his pants. "Okay, I'm through for the day, Miz Davis. Oh, hi, there, Judge Paxton." He greeted the judge with a nod. "Gotta come back sometime tomorrow to finish up the bedrooms, but tomorrow afternoon should do it."

"That's good. Just call Quincee, here, to let you in, please."

"Yes, sir. I'll be on my way, now. My boy's playing baseball tonight, and I promised my wife I'd coach."

"This place is sweltering like a hothouse," Hamilton said as the electrician and his assistant left.

"Yes, it's a scorcher today," Quincee agreed, climbing down from the ladder one last time. She wanted nothing more than to head straight home for a cool bath. "Well, I'm through here. We may as well run along home, too. Shall I rehang these drapes before we go?"

"No, don't bother, Quincee. I'll just dispose of them and have a service come out to hang something new." He couldn't let her go without an acknowledgment of all the extra work she'd done. "The windows look very nice, Quincee. And you've dusted, haven't you?"

A streak of something, grease, he thought, swiped across one cheek, highlighting her freckles. He had a funny yen to tip her face up and wipe it—a yearning to touch her.

"I helped," Kerri said, reminding him the children were present.

"Me, too," Kyle added. "We couldn't vacuum, though, 'cause of no electricity."

Hamilton studied the children. Sweat glistened on Kerri's upper lip, and Kyle had dirty sweat streaks across his forehead. After only a few minutes in this stifling heat, he wanted to pare his own clothes down to nothing but shorts and T-shirt, and these three had suffered in it all day.

"You've done a fine job, too," he said decisively. "Well, I certainly didn't expect all this. I think our bargain deserves a little something extra from my side of it to balance out. How about we go out for supper? Someplace cool.''

"Really?" Kyle's eyes lit up while Kerri grinned.

"That's kind of you, Hamilton, but it isn't necessary," Quincee said. It seemed to him she held her breath in as much delight at the possibility as the children. Would so simple a treat mean so much to her?

Yes, it would, he realized. But her gaze sparkled with something more, something like sweet wonderment, a bit like what he saw in Kerri's eyes.

Why that tickled him, he couldn't imagine. Or dare to think much about. He only knew he wanted to hold on to that spark of excitement between them for as long as possible.

"Oh, but it is," he insisted, and smiled at her. "Can't have my little buddies melting into a puddle of butter at my feet in this heat, now can I?" he said, as he tried a bit of teasing. Something at which he wasn't much good—but then he hadn't had a lot of practice.

He glanced at Quincee from the corner of his eye to gauge her response. The children's giggles encouraged him. "And I sure don't want to lose my best help because I ignore giving good benefits, now do I? And if you ask me, this crew needs a good supper and a relaxing evening out of the heat."

"We'd be delighted," Quincee accepted. "But we—"

"Yay!" Kyle yipped, leaping onto a small footstool and then down again, marching a circle around them. Kerri followed her brother's example, adding her own little skip to the routine.

"—have to clean up first," Quincee completed her directive. "Kyle, you're first in the tub."

"Suits me," Hamilton replied, chuckling at the way Kyle shot out of the room. "An hour?"

"An hour's fine," Quincee replied as Kerri tugged her to follow Kyle. "We'll meet you out front."

Chapter Eight

Hamilton drove them to a country restaurant that featured all-you-could-eat fried chicken and catfish. Hamilton ordered a combination platter. Bowls of vegetables and hot breads came with regularity, giving the children cause for wonder. They munched though their dinners with all the enthusiasm of little birds—eating twice as much as their weight and three times as much as usual.

Quincee and Hamilton talked of the money the rare book dealer had offered for the comic books. "We haven't made a decision to sell them, yet," Quincee told him. She firmed her mouth. "But I think we must. It will go into the children's education fund."

"What do you think of that, Kyle?" Hamilton asked.

"It's okay. Quincee said I can have twenty-five

dollars of it on my birthday to spend on whatever I want.''

''That's a fine idea,'' he said, shooting an approving smile toward Quincee. She didn't know why his approval pleased her so much, but it did.

Her spirits unaccountably soared, and she smiled back. He appeared much younger all of a sudden, his eyes warmer. She liked what she saw there. A lot. In addition, she thought he liked looking at her, too.

She'd have to find a way to provoke more of his smiles.

''I have a special penny,'' Kerri said, looking for her share of attention.

''You do?'' Hamilton shifted his gaze to the little girl.

''Uh-huh. It's got an Indian on it. Quincee said we'd find out if that man will give me more money for it, like Kyle.''

''Excellent, Kerri. You're never too young to appreciate the value of things.''

Kerri beamed under Hamilton's praise. Quincee thought privately that Kerri's real treasure lay in Hamilton's affection.

''Are you ready for dessert?'' The waitress paused in her bustle long enough to ask, then turned toward the children. ''Did you save room for ice cream?''

''Can we?'' Kyle begged while Kerri's blue eyes beseeched.

''Kyle, your tummy is as round as a melon now. If you eat another bite you'll explode. You'll have a stomachache.'' Quincee hated to dash their hopes, but she knew the children's limits. And Kerri had just recovered from being ill. "Thanks," she said to the waitress. "Maybe next time."

Kyle's face fell. Kerri, already slumping in her chair, simply sighed.

"We never get ice cream," the boy grumbled.

"Oh, Kyle, yes, you do," Quincee protested, heat flushing her cheeks. But she felt guilty; sure enough, she'd pared their food budget to the bare essentials. She'd had nothing left over the last three months for special treats—even ice cream. Then, noticing the slight pucker of Hamilton's forehead, she explained, "Our fridge's freezer doesn't hold well enough to keep ice cream firm. That's one of the reasons... never mind. Perhaps I can bargain—er, find a good repair service."

Under the table she pinched her thumb, a small reminder not to spill all her troubles. She already knew the old refrigerator was well past the repair stage. But a new one would have to wait until fall. Maybe even until Christmas.

Hamilton lowered his chin, his steady gaze telling her there would be more complete explanations coming or he'd know the reason. His judge look, she silently called it.

She heaved a big sigh—which only made his eyes narrow. But the sparks leaping in those gray depths weren't all judicial.

"I'll tell you what," Hamilton said, turning to the children without further consultation. "I'm stuffed, just like you, Kyle. So why don't we save our ice cream for tomorrow night? We'll enjoy it more then when we're not so full. All right?''

Kyle brightened. "Okay."

"That's a lovely promise, Hamilton, but you don't have to, really."

"Of course not. But I like ice cream as much as anyone, and it's supposed to be another scorcher tomorrow. Besides, the kids earned it."

"All right."

They still had a couple of hours of daylight left when they returned. "Are we going to work in the garden now?" Kyle asked.

"Oh, for an hour or so, I expect. Need to water the plants."

"I think Kerri and I will take a stroll around the block," Quincee said. "There are a few families on the next street who have signed up for the sale but who haven't made it to one of Bette's meetings. I want to meet them and make sure no one has any unanswered questions."

"But Quincee, I want to help Hamilton," Kerri protested, her brow puckered.

The child had been a bit clingy since her illness. She'd asked for Hamilton a dozen times today, had insisted on sitting beside him at dinner. Glancing his way, Quincee wondered if Hamilton noticed how much Kerri doted on him.

"I know you do, Kerri bear, but I hear that one of the families around the corner have children just about your age." Nearby playmates their own age would be a godsend, she thought. They hadn't had other children to play with since school let out. "Wouldn't you like to come along and see?"

Kerri tipped her head, clearly torn in her choice.

"Why don't you go along with your aunt," Hamilton suggested, "and when you return you may come and say good-night before you go to bed. Will that do?"

"Uh-huh," Kerri agreed.

Quincee glanced at her watch. "We'll be back in about an hour."

It was closer to ninety minutes by the time she and Kerri peeked around the corner of Hamilton's house toward the garden patch. The evening light had waned to dusk, and fireflies decorated the hedges with starlike flashes.

They found Hamilton and Kyle lounging on the back steps of the big house, the screened back porch behind them, sipping from large glasses of ice water. A tray with a pitcher of water, slices of lemon floating on the top, and extra glasses sat between them.

"Did you have a nice visit?" Hamilton asked. He poured them each a glass of water.

"Yes, very nice," Quincee answered, sipping. "They're a nice family."

"And did you make friends with the children?" he asked Kerri, handing her a glass.

Kerri accepted her water, then said indifferently, letting her disappointment show, "Boys."

Kyle looked up. "Yeah?"

"Chip and Danny. They have bikes."

"Oh." He shrugged a shoulder.

"And skateboards."

"Well, I'm going to buy a skateboard with my twenty-five dollars," Kyle boasted, his mouth set in determination. "We can take turns."

Quincee made no comment, but her heart caught on a ragged edge. When was she to afford a few extra pleasures for the children? She didn't blame them for wanting what other children had. They'd gone without for a long time, long before Paula's final illness. And she didn't even have money for ice cream before her next paycheck.

At least she had the neighborhood sale coming, an unexpected boon compared to their situation a month ago. She daren't count her commissions or barter position before the big day, but with any luck, perhaps she'd put new bikes at the top of her A list. After all, there was a lot of summer still to come.

Luck? Blessings, she corrected herself.

Thank you, Lord. Whatever comes from this yard sale, I know You arranged it. I know You'll keep us until I get paid again.

"There's nothing wrong with dreaming," she told Kyle with a smile. "Especially when it's bedtime."

"Aw…" Kyle groaned. "Not yet, Quincee. It's summer."

"Uh-huh, I know you hate to go to bed, tiger. But tomorrow is another day. And remember, we have another day's work tomorrow for the judge, here. We need to be up early."

"That's right, blame me for an early bedtime," Hamilton complained with a deep chuckle. "I'm with Kyle. Summers should mean freedom from strict bedtimes.''

His teasing laughter sent the funniest quiver up her spine; she enjoyed the sensation right down to her toes. She peered at him through the scant light, noting the soft curve of his mouth, the droop of his eyes. She'd never seen Hamilton so relaxed and knew his spontaneous laughter to be rare.

He leaned against the porch post, his long-fingered hands loosely holding his empty glass against a jeans-clad thigh. Left alone, she thought he might drift into sleep right there.

''And how late did you stay up last night, Hamilton?'' she asked only half playfully. ''I noticed your lights still on when I turned ours off after eleven. You look as though you could do with an early night, yourself.''

''Mmm...I refuse to answer on the grounds it may incriminate me.'' Amusement laced his voice. ''But I promise...''

''Yes?''

''Earlier than last night.''

''Cop-out,'' she murmured low, laughing. She rose, holding out her hand for the children to join her. ''We'll be here early in the morning.''

''Fine. But don't exert yourself tomorrow as you did today. There's no need.''

''Um, that might be arguable. Actually, I'd like to get my hands on your parlor. That wallpaper...''

''Oh? How would you change it?''

''I'd lighten it, for sure. Pull off that dark paper

and use a creamy paint, with lots of color in the furniture.'' She descended the three porch stairs, the children following. Then, stopping a few feet away, she turned. "Say, Hamilton, I'm good at painting. Honestly, I could do your parlor. The whole inside.''

"I'm sure you're very good, Quincee, but I don't think I'm ready for that upheaval just now.''

"Well, all right. But you shouldn't let it go too long, you know. Later in the summer, maybe.''

"I'll keep it in mind.''

She started across the yard, listening to his voice float behind her. She stopped and turned.

"You know, we could find a point of trade, I'm sure. You know all about the law. You're part of the system.''

"Don't go there, Quincee.'' His tone stiffened.

"All right,'' she answered, not noticing his offended stance. "But I could use some professional advice at times, and I wouldn't feel obligated for asking a favor if you'd let me—''

"I don't trade my influence or my good name, Miss Davis.''

She suddenly realized he sounded as sober as when he sat on the bench, and just as stiff. She'd offended him. Again. Only this time, she'd insulted him, as well.

And then it hit her how her offer had sounded to him.

"Oh. Oh my goodness! I meant nothing like that, Hamilton,'' she hastened to say. "I didn't mean anything illegal or underhanded, or even in shades of gray. Not at all. Please believe me, Hap. How could you think—''

''It's a hazard I have to guard against.''

''I'm sorry, Hamilton. Really, I wouldn't ask such a thing from you or anyone. I assure you I was thinking of something else entirely.'' Kerri tugged on her hand, while Kyle was already near the hedge. ''We can talk about it later. There's lots of services to barter, and I'd enjoy doing your parlor just for the fun of it.''

''Good night, Quincee,'' he said in dismissal.

''Good night, Hamilton. Thank you again for dinner.''

He made no move to enter his home, standing stiffly sentinel as Quincee and the children traipsed across his clipped, well-cared-for lawn to their dandelion patch.

Long after the children slept, Quincee lay staring out her window, gazing at the glow of lights streaming from Hamilton's library windows. She hadn't meant to offend him, she'd only meant…

What had she been thinking? Of course he'd think the worst; there wasn't much he did approve about her. He thought her an airhead.

Much to her own disgust, that didn't stop her from caring about him just the tiniest bit. As though he needed her input into his life. Not likely. He was fully grown, and it was his choice to live alone. So what, that she detected moments of loneliness he couldn't hide?

She rolled away from the window and closed her eyes. Beside her, Kerri slept soundly.

Quincee had enough on her own plate to think about besides concerning herself with the emotional state of her next-door neighbor. The sale loomed, coming on Saturday. Thank goodness, since it was the Saturday before July fourth, the neighborhood's majority vote had been to hold the sale for only one long day instead of the two or three offered by many other neighborhoods. Once it was over, they could count the profits, and she'd consider making friends of her neighbors her highest blessing. But she did hope she'd earn enough cash from her garage treasures to cover the cost of paint.

Then there was the matter of tracing down the children's father. For their sake, she ought to try to find him. What might happen then, she usually refused to think about. Whenever she did entertain thoughts of finding Mac Stillman, of the outside chance of him wanting custody of Kyle and Kerri, it sent her every nerve into spasms of fear. What would she do if that ever happened? Paula had begged her to raise them, and she loved them with every fiber of herself. But what would her legal rights be?

Flipping onto her back, she stared at the squares on her ceiling made by the reflecting streetlight two doors away. From there, she was drawn once more to check Hamilton's window. Light streamed out. It did seem to her that Hamilton had no one to care about him, to see that he got enough sleep. Didn't the man have a girlfriend?

His lights went out, and moments later, a softer glow appeared from his bedroom window. Five minutes, then all went dark. Her bedside clock showed eleven-fifteen. Sighing, she closed her eyes.

She'd seen no sign of a girlfriend.

Bette had told her Hamilton dated sporadically, but she'd never known the man to be serious about anyone. He seemed to live mostly for his work. Just maybe, on a personal level, the man was shy?

That would be the day.

She needed to concentrate on her own problems, Quincee decided. Perhaps she'd try once again to find the children's father.

Not tonight, her tired mind whispered as she finally relaxed. Instead, she listened to a replay of Hamilton's deep chuckle, recalling the delightful tingles it gave her. Now those were the kinds of shivers of which she'd gladly seek more.

The next day, the electrician finished before noon. Quincee thanked him, and giving a last longing glance at the parlor, locked the judge's house and went home.

She made two more Trash and Treasures posters and sorted through stacks of too-small children's clothing, pricing them. Randolf knocked on her door about four.

Kerri answered the door.

"Come to ask you a favor," he said, coming through with a cardboard box under his arm. "Don't know how to price this stuff."

"What is it?" Quincee asked, glancing up.

"It's fancywork my wife and her mother used to make. I gave lots of it to my daughter-in-law, but she's got all she wants. I have more'n enough clutterin' up my kitchen cabinets an' I don't never use it."

"Oh..." Quincee caught her breath. From the box she pulled a hand-embroidered tablecloth edged with hand-crocheted lace. Beneath that lay matching napkins and a set of seven flour sack tea towels, hand stitched and embroidered, each sporting a day-of-the-week theme. "Mr. Bader, this is lovely work. Are you sure you want to sell them?"

"Don't use 'em." He appeared pleased with her compliment. "Denise would like to know someone was getting some good outta them."

"I have a friend who would love these," she remarked as she gave them a last inspection. "Someone I teach school with who would pay top dollar. Would you mind if I gave her a call tonight?"

"Nah, it's fine with me. Have to say, I'm downright excited with tomorrow coming up. Say, you still want my old piano?"

"Yes, of course. But we must come to some agreement as to the price. May I come and look at it?"

"Sure 'nuff, but I thought you said we'd use it for barter. Want to come now?"

"Yes, now's a good time. But I'm sure the piano will be worth more than what you owe me for my work here, Randolf. Wait a minute so I can lock up the house and gather the kids.''

"Okay."

He shook his head as they strolled across to his house, the children running ahead. "Time was when no one bothered to lock a door just to go see a neighbor. Sad times to think we're not as safe as we once was."

"True enough, Randolf. That's why I pray each morning and evening for the Lord's protection over Kyle and Kerri."

They entered the Bader house, built on the same plan as hers, but newer and with larger rooms. It had the shabby comfortable look of long use. An aging black cocker spaniel hopped down from a chair and nosed Kyle's hand for attention.

"That's Miss Jett," Randolf told the children. "She was my wife's dog."

While the children folded down on the floor to pet the dog, Quincee spotted the upright piano against one wall. Several pieces of sheet music lined the rack as through someone had just left it.

"Are you sure you want to trade this away?" she asked, her heart tugging with nostalgia for the older man. The piano was a good one, and she imagined many pleasurable hours spent on this piano bench. She folded back the keyboard cover and fingered middle C.

"Yeah. Can't stand the thought of it just sittin' here with no one to play it. Denise would like it that some kids were learning music on it. Needs tuning."

"Well, I'm sure it is worth much more than what you'll owe me in commissions." Behind her, she heard Kerri cooing to the cocker as she would one of her dolls. "Would you be willing to take payments in the fall?"

"Could do that. But I been thinking on it. I like playing checkers. Lost my checker buddy when Hamilton's granddaddy went. Kyle, d'you want to spend some of your time this summer with an old man and a checkerboard? I'll help you sand those bicycle fenders, too. And Miss Jett, here, needs someone to pet and play with her once in a while. Wondered if Kerri would do that."

Kyle and Kerri looked to Quincee for an answer. "I think you've got yourself a trade, Mr. Bader."

Chapter Nine

During the night, a shuddering roll of thunder woke Quincee with a start. A second later, a jagged flash of lightning followed. She leaped to her knees, closing her window just as sheets of rain began. Some of it spattered the front of her summer sleep shirt, making it cling, dampening her skin.

Oh, no, why now? What would they do if they were rained out? Nine families were counting on this yard sale. She should have thought of contingency plans.

She rushed into Kyle's room and closed his window, her thoughts hopping from worry to worry. Would enough people come? Could they use garages to showcase their sale goods?

There weren't enough real garages in the old neighborhood to shelter or showcase everything. Besides, it would be impossible to shift it all. She welcomed the cool air that wafted through the house after days of near record heat, but if the rain continued, she saw little hope for a successful sale. They would have to cancel.

Checking every window, she paused to stare out at the street from the living room window. The rain sheeted down. How long would this last?

Then she scolded herself. How could she complain? They needed the rain.

Hadn't Hap complained his garden was dry? He'd turned his lawn sprinklers on for a while every night this week, and she'd let Kyle and Kerri shower their patch of dandelions and grass with the hose.

It wouldn't be the end of the world to postpone the sale. But—she sighed in discouragement—the first enthusiasm and initial thrust would be lost. But maybe they'd luck out and the storm would blow over by morning.

"Quincee?" Kerri's squeak was nearly drowned by another thunderous clap.

"It's all right, Kerri bear," she said, rushing into her bedroom. She sank onto the mattress and placed an arm around her niece. Before she could finish speaking, Kyle sprang onto their bed and folded his legs under him, cuddling under her other arm.

Kyle would never admit to being scared. Only his actions spoke for him.

"It's merely a thunderstorm," she murmured, hugging the children. "My grandma used to say— that would be your great-grandma Molly—well,

Grandma Molly used to say that was the heavenly potato wagon rolling, spilling potatoes as it goes."

They listened to another thundery rumble, not as loud.

"Come on, let's tell stories till we go back to sleep," she said, settling them down one either side of her. It wouldn't be long until Kyle would be too old to cuddle with the girls, she mused. She'd just enjoy these times as long as she could. "What will it be this time?"

"David and Goliath," Kyle begged with relish.

"Cinderella," Kerri insisted.

"Well, let's do the David story. Kyle hasn't had a choice for a while." She cleared her throat and let another heavenly growl roll away before starting. "Now in a long-ago time, Israel came up against a great army. The enemy had a giant in their front ranks, and all the enemy soldiers were jeering at Israel's men, challenging them to fight Goliath. Everyone was afraid of this mean bully. He was a scary dude. But see, God had a plan. Now there was this shepherd boy named David...."

As the children drifted back to sleep, she glanced at her bedside clock. Nearly four-thirty. Her alarm was set for five. She may as well get up.

Carrying her clothes into the bathroom, Quincee dressed and headed toward the kitchen with a huge yawn. She made instant coffee and toast and took them into the living room, maneuvering around boxes of books and old records, of kitchen odds and ends and of the old pink dishes that matched a partial set of Randolf Bader's. They took up most of the available floor space.

She and Randolf had great hopes for those pink dishes.

Sinking into the corner chair, she propped her bare feet on a box. She and Randolf had agreed to share table space and duties. He and Kyle would man their tables, set up along her front sidewalk to display their goods, while she made troubleshooting rounds to the various participants. She'd do her part at their tables when she could.

The nine families had teamed up to share five locations. It was a good plan, she thought.

If the sale weren't canceled. She listened to the steady rain and sighed with disappointment. Everyone had worked so hard. The event seemed to have brought neighbors together in a way that hadn't been done in years.

But she couldn't give up yet. *Lord, I can do all things through Christ Who strengthens me. So I need a little help here*....

She sipped her coffee, checking her list of to-dos before eight this morning. From what she'd heard, they would have their first customers by eight even when they'd listed to begin at nine.

First off, she needed to make tuna salad and have it ready for a quick lunch. She hopped up and hurried into the kitchen, then put eggs on to boil. She set her timer, then returned to the living room and her coffee.

Next, pack her carryall. Her cell phone—a neces-

sity during the months of Paula's illness—went into
the outside pocket; she'd written her number on cards
for each family. If there was a problem, anyone could
reach her quickly. In red, she'd included the numbers
for the police, fire, and ambulance service.

Extra pencils, a couple of pads of paper, rolls of
change, price stickers, a pocket calculator, her permit...

Beyond the sound of the rain, a light tap on her
front door startled her. Five o'clock. Dawn had only
begun to struggle through the heavy clouds.

She hit the front light switch. Peeking cautiously
through the door window, she recognized Hamilton's
tall figure. His dark hair lay plastered to his forehead,
while the back looked blown and bedraggled. His
concerned gaze searched hers under puckered brows.
She yanked open the door.

"Hamilton, what is it? Is there an emergency?"

At her beckon, he stepped through, folding his
dripping umbrella, sticking his flashlight in his back
pocket. He ran his fingers across his wet face and
smoothed his hair away from his eyes.

Quincee lifted her hand, a sudden desire to do that
for him, to smooth his hair and touch his face in
tenderness, shot through her with all the power of a
lightning shaft. His searching gaze went right to her
heart.

"That's what I came to ask you. Is Kerri all right?
Is she sick again?"

"Hmm? No, no. Kerri's fine. Kyle's fine. They're
asleep." Was she? Was she asleep and dreaming

how dear his face had become, how much she wanted to place her palms on either side of his jaw and pull him toward her?

"I saw your light on and I—" Open relief flooded his face with that curious light that sometimes sparked his eyes. "Why are you up so early?"

"The storm." She wished he'd been here earlier. To help comfort the children, of course.

"Ah, yes. I wondered. Hoped it was only that. You are all right then?" He let his gaze slide down her, noting her rumpled looks. "No leaks or…anything?"

"None that I know of, thank goodness." She combed her fingers through her hair, knowing it sprang up of a morning before it was brushed, wondering how badly it looked. "Though I know this house has had leaks in the past. The kitchen ceiling has stains, and the back bedroom. As long as you're here, would you like coffee?"

"Might as well." He left his umbrella on the tiny rug in front of her door and followed her to the kitchen. He eyed the kitchen ceiling, viewing the stains in question. "Yes, I recall when repairs were done."

"Patchwork at best, no doubt." She lifted the pan of boiling eggs from the back burner and placed her tea kettle there. "Another thing for my top ten list, I suppose. Meanwhile I guess I'll climb up there in a few days and check out the whole roof."

"Roofing is best left to the people who know what they're doing, Quincee."

"Yeah, well..." She ignored his instructive tone and placed a heaping teaspoon of coffee crystals into his mug. "I can do all things through Him Who gives me strength, is my motto."

His lips puckered in a thoughtful study. "Paul's words are ones to live by, certainly, but I don't think he was referring to becoming an expert at all things."

Why he felt obligated to point out the obvious, Quincee could only guess. She poured hot water into his mug, conscious of his watching her every move. "I'm not trying to be an expert at everything."

Just at providing a permanent, livable home full of love and security for two kids whose world this last year had been a roller coaster of hospital visits, insecurity and sadness. Who had lost their mom and had no earthly idea at all of a father's love and attention. She sucked on her bottom lip and handed him his coffee.

No, she didn't hope to be an expert at much. Just at loving with all her might.

Hamilton leaned against the cabinets in her tiny kitchen and glanced about him for sugar. She reached around him for the canister and then stuck a clean spoon into his hand.

For a moment, she was so close he could easily have slipped an arm around her waist, closing those three inches between them. His gaze landed smack in the middle of hers, blue eyes wide. And lingered. Desire shot through him as jagged and hot as the lightning outside.

Her mouth softened and parted, and it came as a genuine shock that she wanted him, too, wished to feel his warmth and closeness as much as he wanted hers. The knowledge wedged between them, surrounding them, sure and demanding.

But the last thing in the world either of them needed right now was to involve themselves in a heavy flirtation with disaster. And how could it be anything else? They were neighbors who had nothing more in common than that. Single adults, unentangled and both healthy.

He yanked his thoughts aside, ruthlessly shuttering them. He was much, much too aware of her feminine charms.

Something in her gaze cooled. A response to what she saw in his?

He let Quincee step away, making herself busy. Her voice faintly wobbled as she said, "Just…I need to learn enough repair work to get by."

"Uh-huh. I've noticed." He tried not to allow his tone to sound too dry. Or too affected.

He concentrated on his coffee, letting the awkward moment dissolve. He stirred, sipped, then added more sugar, watching her while she opened two cans of tuna. He tried to lighten his approach. "Ever hear the phrase 'Jack of all trades but master of none'?"

"Oh, sure. I'm a good teacher and I'm working on a master's in early childhood education." Her hands stilled for just a moment as if a new idea had arrested her thought flow. "Or I was. But I like learning other skills, and now I have this house. I have to learn enough to do a creditable job of…whatever repairs it needs.''

"And what you can't learn you try bargaining for. Ever heard of the legal tender in common use in these United States? Commonly called money?''

"Wonderful commodity to have, I agree.'' She flipped the words over her shoulder with a drop of irony, her eyes flashing with humor. She pulled a sharp knife from the drawer beside him, then proceeded to chop onion with a vengeance. "And if I ever find a professional ball player to marry—he can be a marble champion for all I care, he'd still earn more than a teacher—I may well trade in my bargaining hat. But till then, I'm on my own.''

She lifted her chopping board and she scraped the onion into a bowl.

Outside, a wind gust showered the window above the sink with more rain. A heavy rapping followed.

"What now?'' she muttered, setting down her mixing spoon. She wiped her hands on a paper towel and went to the front door. "It's not even five-thirty.''

Hamilton sipped his coffee and listened from the kitchen. "Oh, hello, Randolf. Come in and have some coffee.''

He grimaced, staring into his mug. He might have known. That old coot Bader had taken quite a shine to Quincee; he'd been hanging around their side of the street ever since she'd moved in. A man of his years should think better of his actions, that's what Granddad would've said.

A small thud caused him to turn toward the door into the back bedroom. The children appeared a moment later, Kerri rubbing her eyes.

"Hiya, Hap," Kyle mumbled. Kerri sidled up to lean against his legs. Without thinking about it, he cupped the child's head, his long fingers stroking her cheek.

"In any case, storm or not," Quincee said with a daunted sigh as she led the old man into the kitchen, "I was slated to be up early this morning because of the sale. I don't know what we'll do now. This rain…"

"TV says it'll be gone by midmorning. Might's well hang on till then. Some'll come even in a downpour."

"I suppose we can try it. I wonder if the others are game?" After all the hard work, she was loath to give up altogether. "We can start out in my living room."

"I don't think that's a good idea, Quincee," Hap said. "Strangers coming into your house? Unchecked? That's asking for trouble."

"I'll contain the sale to the living room," Quincee insisted. "Mr. Bader is here to help."

Spotting the judge, Randolf stopped abruptly, staring from under droopy lids. "Well, my stars, Hamilton, what the hay are you doing here so early this morning? You gonna join us in this here yard sale after all?"

"Wasn't planning on it."

"Go and get dressed," Quincee told the children. "We have lots to do this morning."

"Then what're you doing here?" Bader insisted on an answer.

"Checking on... Never mind." He set his mug on the counter and pushed himself away from it. "Thanks for the coffee, Quincee. I'll go now. But take care and don't do anything really foolish."

He let himself out the back door into the dark morning, the rain pelting him as he started around the house toward the front sidewalk.

"Hamilton..." Quincee opened her front door to call him just as he came even. "You forgot your umbrella."

She came down her two front steps, opening it. He met her on the sidewalk, reaching for it, his hand covering hers.

"Thanks for checking on us, Hamilton. It's sweet of you to worry."

"It's a hazard, I'll admit," he said, wanting again to kiss her, regretting his lost opportunity in the house. Wishing he had the courage to take a simple pleasure at will, in spite of the fact old man Bader watched them from her wide-open door.

Abruptly, he turned and covered the distance to his house in long strides. The wind whipped at his umbrella, splattering his face with rain. He was grateful. It would cool his irritation and his...hunger.

He guessed that after all, he was glad Randolf had arrived.

Desire and lust. He'd always imagined that's how

he'd been conceived. From an easy liaison, as nothing more than a sexual craving easily fulfilled between two careless people. He'd been an unwelcome accident, knowing from a very early age that he'd never allow himself to follow in his father's footsteps.

Under his grandfather's tutelage and a strong sense of God's design for marriage, he hadn't allowed himself to indulge in loose affairs while he was in college. Or since.

He'd be walloped if he'd start now.

No, his idea of a permanent relationship began with a deep friendship, with a lifestyle and interests in common, a bond growing into love over a long period. Not this sudden crushing desire to kiss a saucy mouth until the moon rose on the far side of the earth, or to pander to this out-of-control urge to tuck her under his arm for safekeeping, either.

Maybe it was time he married. But if he intended to wed, perhaps he should first find a feet-on-the-ground girlfriend, someone who traveled in his law circles, who had solid ambitions that matched his.

However, he could admit his opinion about Quincee was rapidly changing. He still thought her too much of a flibbertigibbet, but she was clever enough to push her own hidden agenda.

What was it she actually wanted from him? Was it really only neighborly of her to want to trade chore for chore? Work for work? Or something deeper?

Quincee needed money, she made no secret of it. From what little Kyle had let drop, he was sure they received nothing from the children's father. Maybe that was it. She hoped for his help in forcing the man to pay.

Drat it! He would not leave himself or his position open to be used. There were agencies to track down absentee fathers, courts to settle the issues. None of this was his responsibility.

Yet his anger rose when he thought of his irresponsible parents. It wasn't right, fair or legal for a man to negate his obligations, and Quincee shouldn't have to struggle so hard to make her month fit into an inadequate income.

Perhaps he'd just pursue the matter, after all. Quietly. Quincee needn't know.

Maybe they'd luck out, and the storm would blow over by morning light.

Chapter Ten

The phone began to ring before seven.

"Yes, let's go ahead and try," Quincee answered the first of half a dozen callers. "The radio says the day will clear up in a couple of hours. Until then, let's hang loose and take care of the few people who will come anyway."

"Good thing Bette thought to put that plastic wrap over our signs," Randolf mentioned between rings, hitching up his drooping shorts. They'd lined the streets from the main artery roads with directional signs that read Junk and Jewels, and Trash and Treasures.

While she manned the phone, Randolf and the children roped off the doorway into the main part of the house and laid out their various goods on the sofa and a folding table.

"It's too bad that my garage is still too jumbled

to use,'' she mumbled. Between Kerri's illness and the amount of time she'd spent helping her neighbors classify their goods for sale, she hadn't had time to finish sorting out her garage. ''Next time—if I'm ever crazy enough to do this again—we'll use it.''

The phone buzzed again, and Quincee picked it up. This time it was a shopper. ''Yes, ma'am, we're still holding our sale. We're open for business at nine and have four locations along our block. Just look for the red painted signs to show you which houses.''

Then a neighbor rang with a brilliant solution. ''The tent sounds like a great idea, Jim, if you can get it up in this rain. Yes, Mr. Bader's on his way with the extra stakes you need. You let me know if you need anything else.''

Punching the off button, she glared at the phone, daring it to ring one more time. Outside, clouds filtered a gloomy morning light, but the rain had lightened, thank heaven.

''Quincee, there's a car out front,'' Kerri said from the window. She had grape jam on her cheeks, and she left a smear of it decorating the windowpane. ''A lady is coming to the door.''

Quincee nearly groaned. She sent the children to the kitchen to finish their breakfast. ''And make sure you wash your hands and faces, please.''

''Hello,'' the woman said through the screen door, giving a quick, professional smile. She was a stylish woman, about fifty, with an air of having done this many times, but she carried no purse. ''I do hope you're ready. Sorry to arrive so early, but I have to work today and I didn't want to miss this sale. Your ads were so inviting.''

Quincee had been told that the antique store buyers, wanting their best bargains, did an early garage sale crawl.

''Ah, well, you're only fifteen minutes early. We officially open at nine.'' She could be gracious, Quincee decided. The sale should be as easy for customers as possible.

As Quincee swung her door wide, another car passed slowly, the driver craning his neck to see what was happening. He parked his car in front of the woman's and came across the wet yard, disregarding the sidewalk.

''How's business?'' he asked by way of greeting. His face fanned out in many lines, the ones bracketing his eyes running into graying hair at his temples. He didn't wait for Quincee to open the door. He did that for himself and strode in, but thoughtfully wiped his shoes on the small rug in front of the doorway. He tossed a brassy grin at the other visitor. ''Hiya, Janice. Fancy meeting you here.''

Quincee thought he, too, knew how to go about shopping at yard sales.

He began to look around at the goods, hands in his pockets, all the while half watching what the woman, Janice, was doing. Janice tried hard to ignore him.

Outside, Quincee heard a sudden shout. She peeked through the window.

"Uh-oh. No...don't, please," she muttered under her breath. "Not on Hamilton's lawn."

Too late. A large teal van had parked half on the street and half on Hamilton's perfectly kept green lawn. The driver had one foot out the van door. Hamilton stood on his sidewalk, waving the driver to move off, and by his body language, Quincee didn't think he was a happy camper.

The driver seemed prone to argue. Both his feet hit the street. She sucked her breath and held it. She couldn't hear what Hamilton said, but a glimpse of his scowl would cause King Kong to tremble.

He'd scare all the customers away.

He'd say I told you so and be justified.

He'd lay all his frustration at her feet.

Whirling from the front window, she wove her way through the litter and goods on display toward the front door. She'd better do something, and quick. The last thing she needed was Hamilton's dander flaring red at her again.

Then on an intake of breath, she remembered. She couldn't leave her post while Randolph ran his errand. Like a rubber band being stretched and then let go, she bounced back to gaze out the window.

The van was driving off. Quincee watched it out of sight with a slow sigh. Where was Hamilton now?

"Miss? These pink dishes?" Janice the customer asked.

Quincee swung away from the front window just as a noisy honk blasted the air, and gritting her teeth, she tried not to think about Hap.

The pink dishes? What had Mr. Bader said they were worth? She'd merely placed a sticker on them to reflect the bottom line of what he thought they'd bring.

"Um...I..."

"Is your price on them firm?" The woman asked.

"Well, I think they're worth at least the sticker price." And more, according to Mr. Bader.

"One of the big plates has a chip," the woman pointed out with disdain. "I'll give you fifteen dollars for the lot."

The woman reached into her pocket and pulled out a roll of bills the size of a fist. She peeled off a ten and a five.

"Does it? Oh, I'm sorry," Quincee answered uncertainly. She'd thought all the pieces she and Randolf had placed in the sale were in good condition. "But I really must wait until Mr. Bader comes back before cutting down the price to less than half. He thought the price already low, you see."

The gentleman customer snickered, then glanced away.

"All right. How about twenty-five?" the woman insisted, her chin thrust out.

"Ah..." Usually, Quincee thought herself a woman of quick decisions, but just then Hamilton yanked open her door and strode through, sending all her thoughts scattering like chicks from a fox. She could no more give the woman a cogent answer than climb a ladder to the moon.

"Quincee!" he yelped, his gray eyes blazing with

ire. Rain dripped off his tan rain hat, depositing a big splash of wet on his nose. His mouth tightened. "If you don't do something—"

Yet the shivers his gaze sent over her struck no fear in Quincee, not even jitters. Only sparks of...sweet amusement. The kind of humor one feels all mixed up with love and affection and tender indulgence for a friend. Or someone much loved.

"Here I am, Hamilton," she said, surprising herself with the calmness she suddenly felt. She stepped forward, knowing some of her emotion tugged at her mouth. "What's the problem?"

Hamilton scrutinized her expression for only a moment. She couldn't tell if he wanted to personally wring her neck or stomp the floor, but behind his eyes, his ire softened. "Parking!"

He spotted the two customers and clamped his mouth tight, the line bringing creases into his cheeks, his gaze flashing with what she thought of as rueful apology.

"Morning, Judge Paxton." The gentleman customer spoke.

"Morning, Mr. Riley. You here to see if my young friend has any more comic books for sale?" He gave an acknowledgment to the children standing in the doorway, both wide-eyed with curiosity.

"Thought it a good idea to check things out," Mr. Riley said with a nod toward Quincee. "How you doing, young fella?" he asked Kyle before turning back to Hamilton. "Nice to see you this morning. I didn't realize you lived in this neighborhood."

"Yes, I grew up on this street." Hamilton turned to the woman. "And Janice Locks, I see. You're out early for business this morning."

The woman's smile had an ironic twist as she flashed a quick, oddly curious glance Quincee's way before answering Hamilton. "Your famed memory for faces always astounds me, Judge Paxton. I'd wager you know every merchant on the square and beyond, just as your grandfather did."

"I know a few of them, sure enough," he replied. "You still have that antique shop? If I recall, you do a brisk business in china and glassware, don't you?"

The woman smiled, then dug into her stash of bills again to peel off another twenty-five dollars. "All right, forty it is," she said, placing the full sticker amount into Quincee's palm. "Hamilton, you aren't helping my cash flow a'tall, you hear? Bye, now. Gotta go make a few more rounds."

Mr. Riley chuckled. Hamilton merely raised his brows.

"Sorry, Mr. Riley," Quincee said. "We haven't had time to look for more comic books, but if we have any, Kyle knows where we can find you."

"Fair enough."

Hamilton saw the customers out, remaining on the front sidewalk to chat with Mr. Riley. Then Mr. Bader came back.

"Randolf," Quincee said, gathering her heavy felt-tip pens and a couple of empty cardboard boxes from the dining room, "watch things for a bit, will you? I have to do something for Hamilton."

She made two No Parking signs, quickly stapled them to stakes from a stack she and Bette had used for that purpose, and carried them out to Hamilton just as the two store owners pulled away.

"Here. Stick these at your curb," she instructed. "That should solve the problem."

"Maybe," he said with a dash of disgust, staring at the deep tire gashes in his lawn. "But people don't always pay attention to signs. As you should know."

"Guess that's true," she returned slowly, feeling a shaft of hurt. "But there are signs and there are signs."

Was she still on probation with the judge? He'd scolded her that first time when she came before him in traffic court for ignoring No Parking signs. She believed in obeying society's rules, but she'd had good reason to ignore the demands of traffic that day. She'd never had an opportunity to explain her actions, and now that they'd grown to being friends, she'd put all that behind her. Somehow, she hadn't expected him to throw her past infringement in her face.

"Quincee..." A note of apology deepened his tone, but she turned away as a truck came even with them. She plastered on a smile and waved the driver to park in her driveway.

After that, the morning seemed to blur into a whirlwind of visitors. She scarcely noticed when the rain ceased. Her plan to make a round to all the sale sites leached away as she couldn't seem to pull Randolf away from the talkers. But when she could, she kept in touch with each family by phone.

Just before noon, she left Randolf and the children in charge and made a run up the street in the opposite direction from Hamilton's house. She stopped to chat a moment with each sale participant, finishing her round at Gene and Bette's house.

Approaching the last leg of the block, which brought her opposite of hers and Hamilton's home, she slowed her steps. She ignored the fact that cars came and went and, as with any yard sale, pulled into and out of positions along the street. She'd waved and greeted quite a few customers, stopping to make them feel welcome.

But now she noticed there were cars in front of Hamilton's house, too. Again. Hadn't her No Parking signs worked for him?

She couldn't look. Instead she kept her gaze on the Longacres, congenially chatting with someone they seemed to know.

But she couldn't ignore the problem, either. How angry was he? What could she do to make it right with him later?

Make him a pie? Offer to clean his house next week? Do his mending?

Then she grinned. She'd have her driving privileges back this week. She'd offer to do his household errands. Now wouldn't he just love that? But he had complained he hated that mundane chore. Perhaps she'd even bring him wallpaper samples to quicken his enthusiasm for redoing his parlor.

She greeted Gene and Bette. "How's it going, folks?"

"Doing pretty good," Gene Longacre crowed as she stepped upon their porch. "Made almost a hundred dollars this morning in spite of the rain."

"Yes, and Hamilton has been of great help, bless him," Bette said as she saw her customers down their front steps.

"What do you mean?" Quincee asked, her tummy doing a dip, totally unrelated to being hungry.

"Why, look at him," Bette responded with a nod to direct her gaze across the street.

Biting her lip, Quincee slowly turned. Then opened her mouth. Hamilton stood under his rain hat, directing a car as it backed out of his driveway. Then he waved another into his driveway, speaking a moment with the driver as she got out.

"What is he doing?" The words squeaked out.

While she watched, he guided a truck and another car in perfect alignment against his curb. She saw no signs of any kind.

"He's been directing traffic all morning. See, there are customers in our drive, too."

Bette went to stand on the edge of her front porch to greet the three women ascending the steps as though they were honored guests. "Come on up, ladies. Look around. I still have some nice costume jewelry in that box. If you need help, I'll be right here."

The traffic lulled. Quincee started down the Longacre steps and beelined across the street, her gaze glued to Hamilton; he'd made an effort to help by way of an apology, she just knew it.

He stood at the edge of his drive. He wasn't smiling, but he didn't appear as grim as earlier, either.

"Hamilton?"

"Yes?" He lifted a brow and gave her a quizzical, half suspicious glance.

Without a single preconceived notion, Quincee stepped close to his tall, rangy body, rose to her toes, placed her hands against his angular cheeks and pulled his face down to hers.

She kissed him.

Smack on his mouth.

Against her palms, his unshaven jaw teased her skin. She stroked his jaw with her thumb, feeling the rasp of his day's growth, which quickened her heartbeat in seductive response. Her lips went soft against his, and she let them stay a moment, feeling dizzy with the buzz that went to her head and the weakness that shot to her knees.

Slowly, she sank down from her toes. By inches she withdrew her hands and her lips, murmuring "Thank you. Thank you."

He sucked in air like a man with no oxygen supply at all and stared at her as though she'd hit him with a brick.

The buzz stayed with her. Spinning on her heel, she half ran, her heart beating wildly. With each step, her speed increased.

She raced past the children, hopscotching along the front sidewalk.

She ran past Randolf, standing on her front walk, his old blue eyes roundly surprised.

She ran until she was inside her house with the door closed behind her. There she drew a deep breath and caught herself just before it escaped in a groan.

Now what had she done? And in front of all the neighbors, too.

They officially closed the sale at three. True to predictions from a couple of her new friends, Quincee had noticed the rapid decrease of customers during the early part of the afternoon. Since this was the Saturday before July fourth, she knew many people had already left town for the lakes.

She and Randolf packed away all the remaining goods, and then they all strolled over to the Longacres'. Gene sat in his porch glider, half asleep.

"Huh. Might a known you were gettin' your nap come hel—help or high waters," Randolf scoffed as he climbed the front steps. To give the older man credit, Quincee had noticed he watched his language around the children. She suspected he could be very colorful in other company.

"I didn't notice you running any races," Gene returned.

Quincee and Bette left the men to banter and went inside to total the final shared costs. The children were content to play a new game they'd found that had cost Quincee a dollar in the sale.

The clouds finally drifted away, and the sun heated what remained of the day. The Tillotsons, a young couple without children who lived half a block down, called to invite all the participants to join them for a spontaneous hamburger supper on their backyard deck.

"Sounds like a plan to me," Quincee said as she and Bette wrapped up their bookkeeping. "I'm way too exhausted to cook."

"Me, too," Bette agreed. "I have some nice macaroni salad I can contribute."

"We have a huge jar of pickles. I'll bring them," Quincee said. "But for the next five minutes I just want to sit."

Thirty minutes later, they all sauntered down the street together. Kerri skipped a few yards ahead, then stopped to wait for them. Kyle already had reached the Tillotsons.

"I must admit we had fun with it, didn't we?" Bette said of the sale. "And we made a hundred and twenty-six dollars and change. I think we'll give it to the church's teen group. They always need financing. Camping and retreats and such."

"That's a wonderful thought," Quincee agreed. "I'll certainly tithe on my proceeds, too. You know, my mom always believed in tithing."

Quincee hadn't thought of that biblical principle in years, but she suddenly resolved to begin to tithe her income. It felt very right; she needed to do this.

She realized how much she looked forward to attending church tomorrow, too. She longed to stand among others and sing God's praises, to thank Him for this time of blessings. She thought of all the good things that had lined up for her lately.

Kerri had gotten the medical help she needed. Quincee's nondriving period was over, and she hadn't turned blue with frustration. And she'd have a new paycheck in the bank on Monday with which to pay bills. Best of all, she and the kids had found friends in their new neighborhood. It felt like home.

And Hamilton...

She felt her cheeks flush as her thoughts jumped around like Ping-Pong balls. She'd been really foolish.

Oh, Lord, what am I going to do about all this embarrassment I've brought down on my own head?

Yet her heart fluttered when she thought of his mouth and how it felt on hers.

Chapter Eleven

Hamilton, just out of his shower, sorted through his closet for something to wear. A dark blue T-shirt, cargo shorts and sandals would do for a neighborhood gathering, he supposed.

He didn't know why he'd even been invited, or why he'd agreed to have supper at the Tillotsons'. He hadn't been a part of the group effort except by default and under protest. The attending crowd would want to talk about the sale. They'd discuss its better points and debate what they should have done differently, and unless he kept his mouth shut, he'd lend a pall to their satisfaction.

After dressing, he sank onto the small bench beside his front bedroom window to adjust one of his sandals, contemplating the evening before him.

He'd be wiser to call and beg off. He had other things to do with his time on a Saturday night.

Like what? Hole up in the library and work again?

He wasn't in the mood. This last year, he'd spent too many evenings alone. Working, crossing legal *T*s and dotting important *I*s. A reputation for exactness had to be kept up, after all.

That would account for his restlessness, surely. Not that saucy bit of womanhood next door who flaunted her femininity like a white flag conceding surrender. Never mind that bodacious kiss she'd planted on him in front of the entire neighborhood!

What in the great wide universe had the woman been thinking?

Honestly, how was a red-blooded unattached male supposed to react to such a zany female? Ignoring her wouldn't work. He'd already tried that. She was the kind of woman who crawled under a man's skin and dug her way into the bones. He'd tried his usual buffers; they'd worked with other women.

He pushed himself to stand, shoved his wallet into his back pocket and dropped his change into his front pocket, then grabbed his brush and ran it through his hair, twisting his mouth at a half dozen gray hairs he found near his temple. Like Granddad, he guessed, he'd gray early as part of his genetic inheritance. Most people thought him older than he was, anyway. Quincee did.

Lord have mercy! Why should that bother him? Why couldn't he stop thinking about her?

His trouble was, he was beginning to fear Quincee was already under his skin, working her way up to his heart. And that sent alarm bells clanging to his toes. She wasn't the kind of woman he pictured as a life partner. She was too...young for him.

Only by six or seven years...

She too often acted before she thought things through. No predicting what kind of trouble she'd bring him. Yet she already troubled him more than he'd like to admit.

She was too blessed sexy.

Running down his staircase, he felt the echoes of his empty house. He should get out and do something on a Saturday night. Be with people. But maybe he shouldn't put himself in the neighbors' company any more today.

He glanced at his watch. It was a little late to call a friend to meet him for dinner. Besides, this was the first day of a long four-day holiday for many of his usual cohorts. They'd already taken off for the Lake of the Ozarks, Truman Lake, Pomme de Terre or even Branson.

If it weren't so muddy, he could work in the garden—but after today's rain, it would take a day or two to dry out. The grass was too wet to cut. He didn't want to see a movie alone.

Kyle's woebegone request for ice cream came to mind. He'd promised the child they'd have some this weekend. Kerri's captivating trust always tugged at his emotions, too, and he couldn't bear to disappoint the children.

Ruthlessly, he shoved away the image of Quincee's mouth, the feel of how her lips softened beneath his own. He'd been totally rattled, frozen in amazement when she'd kissed him right on the sidewalk.

He'd wanted to kiss her back—she'd felt wonderful against him.

Wouldn't that have given the neighbors a show!

Yet her lips had been so enticing, her palms against his cheek piercingly sweet....

All right! It wouldn't hurt him to join the neighborhood crowd, now, would it? He didn't have to mix with Quincee—only the children. He let out a gusty breath and dug out his car keys. He knew just which ice-cream store had the best product.

An hour later, he arrived at the Tillotsons' with three kinds of ice cream and two kinds of toppings, hot fudge and caramel. Plus nuts, sprinkles, whipped cream and, to top it off, Maraschino cherries.

Hamilton glanced around the backyard. This house had changed hands a couple of years back for the second time since he'd tossed a football around here with Jonsey Smith while they were both in junior high school. The Tillotsons had done a lot of improvement, the lovely wide deck being the best example.

The children sat on a bench against the railing, counting change between them.

He greeted everyone with an inclusive hi and handed Judy Tillotson the bag with the ice cream. Sauntering over to the children, he asked, "Did you make lots of money with your sale?"

"Uh-huh." Kyle glanced up from his stack of quarters to answer with awe. "We have seven dollars and seventy cents. With my twenty-five dollars, maybe I can buy a bike!''

"I want a bike, too," Kerri complained.

"You're too little for a bike. You can have a tricycle.''

"I'm not a baby." Kerri's under lip thrust out. "Only babies have trikes.''

"Well, you're too little to ride in the street and you can't ride a bike on the sidewalk. Can she, Hap?''

"I'm too old for a baby tricycle," Kerri insisted before he could answer, giving Hamilton the thought that the child was learning lessons from her aunt Quincee. "I can ride a bike.''

"We don't have 'nuff money to buy two bikes," Kyle said, his tone plaintive. "It's too hard to save for only one. We'll never have enough money for two.''

Hamilton felt Quincee's presence just behind him, something of her essence reaching out to touch him. Glancing over his shoulder, he caught a sad wistfulness in her eyes, focused on the children. Then she lifted her gaze and realized he watched her; he caught a piercing sense of love and helplessness before she swiftly shuttered her thoughts.

He'd thought he was beginning to know her. Now he realized he didn't know her nearly well enough. She hid her depths beneath layers of outer display.

"We'll settle this later, kids," Quincee said, bending to help the children collect their coins. "Put your money away now. It's rude to quarrel in front of our friends. We're about ready to eat, anyway.''

She turned her attention toward Bette, and Hamilton joined the men around the barbecue grill, helping to hand the hot dogs and hamburger patties over to the women, who placed them on the picnic table. He sat beside Ron Tillotson and listened to the various points of the day as they ate. He joined the discussion only when they veered into generalities of their town or honed into a discussion of local politics.

Neither Gene nor Bette made a reference to Quincee's sidewalk display, nor did Randolf tease, as Hamilton half expected him to do. Yet by an occasional speculative sidelong glance tossed his way, he was sure the incident was neither over nor forgotten, only lying in wait to leap up to surprise when he least expected it.

He'd have to distance himself from Quincee and the children, he thought, ignoring the squeeze that suddenly attacked his heart. When one was a judge and a church deacon, one had to be careful of reputation. Dignity had to be served, as well.

Yet at the close of the evening when it was time to walk the half block home, Kerri slipped her hand into his, her trust in his acceptance pure and unthinking. The child missed having a father. At five, he'd missed having one, as well—except he long ago realized he couldn't miss what he'd never really had.

He bit down on his sudden anger. He still didn't know the whole story of Kyle and Kerri's parentage, but he was becoming increasingly curious. He mentally reviewed the facts he knew. Their mother had passed away. Quincee had the sole care of them, and she was so short of money she barely made ends meet. Except, he suspected, those ends hadn't met for quite a while. She'd hinted as much, mentioning her schoolteacher pay.

Where were these children's father? Why didn't the man pay child support?

Quincee hadn't confided in him on these matters, yet he'd hazard a guess that Stillman hadn't paid up. Hadn't the law caught up with him? Why hadn't the man shown an interest in their whereabouts? Didn't he care about them?

Hamilton could do nothing to force a parent to love their children, but by heaven, he could do something about the child support, and he would. First thing Monday morning. Not all the offices were closed over the four days. There were ways to trace where a delinquent father could be found, and he had the means and contacts to cut some red tape to do it.

He tightened his fingers around the little girl's, feeling the small tender bones beneath his thumb. A gut-wrenching wonder followed over the affection for the child that shot through him. He observed Kyle's boyish enjoyment as he ran in front of Quincee and the Longacres, racing from street lamp to street lamp, then stopping to wait by the one just beyond Quincee's house.

If these were his children, he'd move heaven and earth to take proper care of them.

That was what Quincee was trying to do, he realized. Without whining or complaining. All at once, her gutsy attitude took on new meaning. She wasn't giving an inch to any kind of defeat. In any direction.

Something about that tickled his funny bone. Safely in the dark, he let his grin spread.

He noted the gentle sway of Quincee's hips as she strolled a few feet in front of him. She was a little thing, though he liked the way she filled her clothes. Sometimes he wanted to lift her to stand on a step or a brick so that they could better meet eye to eye while they talked.

Only to talk? That was a laugh. He wanted a great deal more than to talk. When he looked at Quincee he felt more like eighteen than thirty-three, with teenage hormones raging out of control—even when she'd irritated him to the max. What was it about her that set him off?

Kerri tugged at his hand, jerking his thoughts under control. "Hap, I'm tired."

"You are?" He bent to swing her into his arms as they crossed the street to Quincee's house. "I suppose you're still recovering from being ill, and it's been a long day. But we're almost home now. You can snuggle into bed and go fast asleep in no time."

Kyle ran a circle around Quincee and the Longacres, standing where they'd paused to finish their conversation. Halfway into the empty street, Hamilton turned, waiting. Kerri rested her head against his shoulder.

"Say, young fella," Gene said, laying a hand on the boy's shoulder to slow him down. "Are you coming to church tomorrow? There's a couple of boys your age in our Bible class there that would make dandy friends. I know the couple that teaches in that department, and they sure do like young 'uns. Seems I heard something about a picnic going on later in the month after the holiday.''

"Oh, yes, Quincee, do come early enough for the children to attend Bible class," Bette urged. "There's a place for Kerri, too."

"Can we go, Quincee?" Kyle asked.

"Sure, honey. We'll go."

"I'll drive you," Hamilton said on a quiet note, taking a step toward them.

"Thanks, Hamilton, but I'll drive myself." Quincee half turned his way to answer. "There's a few errands I need to take care of as soon as church is over."

"But you can't."

"Yes, I can. My suspension is lifted."

"Ah..." He blinked, a shaft of disappointment slicing through his mind. How could he have forgotten? Had he grown to like her occasional dependency on him? He felt like a dodo, his brains addled by that kiss today.

He had to shake it off.

Quincee said goodbye to the others with the promise to see them in the morning and headed his way, pulling her front door keys from her pocket.

Hamilton turned toward Quincee's house, shame creeping up his spine. As a deacon, he should've thought about enrolling the children in Sunday morning Bible class himself. Not only would the children learn about God and how to relate to Him, but they needed the interaction with other children their own age. Their world was filled with too many adults.

Relationships. The thought churned in his mind. The scripture was full of what went into a right relationship; with God, with family and with others, with a spouse.

He'd been so blessed to have his grandfather. Otherwise, he'd have ended up hating his parents for their abandonment. Granddad had taught him not to hate and instead directed him to follow God's precepts. He didn't hate his parents now—but it had been a long time since he'd thought much about them. If pressed, he would own up to having no respect for them. They'd done nothing to earn it. Nothing at all.

But that didn't remove God's command to honor thy father and mother, did it? The fact that his parents had thoughtlessly created him and then abandoned him at a young age didn't remove God's love from him.

Or from his parents.

An overwhelming need to forgive his parents rushed through him. His father had hated Granddad's rules and strict training, but Hamilton had flourished under them. How could he go on blaming Richard when he'd had Granddad?

And his mother… When she'd turned him over to Granddad, hadn't she been helpless and desperate to provide for him?

God, forgive me…. Wash me of this unforgiveness I've carried so long.

God loved his parents as much as anyone—after all, weren't they among the lost sheep, ones that would send the shepherd out to search for them? God's plan of salvation was there for all.

However, it was their responsibility to accept God's love for themselves, individually. Each must accept Father, Son and Holy Spirit into their lives. It was up to them to take those steps of faith.

But how long had it been since anyone shared that knowledge with them? To follow the Scripture as directed in the Book of Romans. Maybe they needed another opportunity to make that decision.

Perhaps it was time he made an effort at reconnecting with them. A phone call? No… He wasn't ready for that. What could he say when they didn't seem to care that he existed? But a letter could open a dialogue.

Father, he prayed silently, *guide my hand as I write to each of my parents. Only You can prepare their hearts to hear. If they don't respond, then at least I've tried. And I don't want to be caught in an unforgiving trap so that I can't go forward to love properly.*

And give me wisdom as I pursue the whereabouts of these children's father, for I mean to do that. Mac Stillman has to be given the opportunity to become the father You intended Kyle and Kerri to have.

Then as Quincee swung open her door and reached for a drowsy Kerri, and he moved to transfer the child, his arms encircled them both for an instant. A flash of deep, yearning tenderness seemed to run out his fingers right into the skin on Quincee's arms, soft and firm beneath his touch.

He made the drastic mistake of glancing into her blue eyes. An allurement lay there, of which she may or may not be aware, he fleetingly thought, and he sucked in his breath. But he sure enough wanted to follow her right through the door, to linger to see where that sweet feeling would lead.

Thoughts and feelings and scattered emotions tumbled forth like a tornado spitting out all the various goods it had picked up, leaving him in such a state of confusion he couldn't speak.

Oh, Lord, he was in big trouble! If he put one foot across Quincee's threshold tonight, he'd be totally out of control five minutes after the kids were put to bed.

Had he lost his ever-lovin', near-genius mind? God help him, where in the world was his usual staid good sense?

All right, Lord, he prayed, and swallowed hard. *Help…*

Chapter Twelve

~

"Say again? You did what?" Laura gave Quincee her this-is-not-appropriate-behavior stare that sent most of her students into cowering retreat. Then she began a slow, delighted, knowing smile. "That stuffed shirt? What did he do? Say?"

Quincee chuckled in response, then shook her head and sighed. Laura had met them after church, and she'd splurged some of her yard sale cash for lunch. Now they lounged on a park bench watching the children play on the jungle gym and slides.

"He didn't say anything. Just stared at me out of those fantastic eyes of his as though I'd lost my mind." Quincee stretched out her legs and crossed her ankles. "I shouldn't have done it, I'll admit it was stupid. But I... He surprised me by helping so much after all the objections, and I wanted to thank him."

"But Quincee—in front of the neighbors? And what you describe certainly overqualified as a mere thank-you kiss."

"Yeah, it did sizzle a bit," Quincee answered with a tiny prick of smug satisfaction. Feeling embarrassed now would do her no good, she mused. Then remembering how much she'd liked it, liked the warm touch of his lips, she felt her face flush. But she thought he'd liked it, too.

She definitely had dual feelings about her motivation, yet she couldn't admit that to Laura. Not yet, for sure.

"It was totally thoughtless of me, I guess. But it woke him up, at least," she murmured.

"How do you mean?" Laura asked, waving at Kerri who stood at the top of the slide.

"He's so sure of himself about everything in life. Except, I think, dealing with me. He could barely look at me during the barbecue. When he did..."

"What?" Laura's light eyes mirrored her thirsty, amused curiosity.

"Oh, I don't know. He tried to behave naturally, but I could tell that I made him skittish. He hardly knew which way to jump. He still can't make me out, I guess." Quincee wasn't sure she understood herself right at that moment, either. It seemed, looking back, she'd acted without conscious volition. Her urge to kiss him had been overwhelming.

She'd have to cope with why later, Quincee guessed, because Kerri fell just then and skinned her knee. Tucking her confused emotions away, she jumped up to soothe the child.

"Any plans for the Fourth?" she asked Laura as they headed toward their cars.

"Yes, I'm going to visit my parents in Warrensburg for the day. Then I'm doing a concert with friends in the evening. What are you planning?"

"Oh, nothing much. Something fun with the kids that won't cost more than an arm," she said with a chuckle to hide the tiny wave of envy she felt. Last year, she'd found similar activities, running off to a day of carefree enjoyment with friends.

Quincee waved goodbye and took a deep breath as she started the car. Her freedoms had changed, for sure, but she wouldn't trade having the children in her life now for any of it. They were the sunshine of her days, what she had left of her family.

"Quincee, can we go visit Mom again soon?" Kyle asked as she pulled onto Noland Road. Glancing in her rearview mirror, she caught the pensive expression in Kyle's eyes. The request tugged at her heartstrings.

Until she'd lost her driving privilege, Quincee had taken the children to the cemetery almost once a week. She'd encouraged them to talk as though their mother could hear every word, and wiped their tears as they left, cheering them up with an ice cream on the way home.

"Sure, honey." Her voice came out wavery, and she swallowed hard on a sob that wanted to erupt. It would get easier for all of them, and the Lord had promised to see them through all tears and sorrows. "We've got time right now."

"But we don't have a flower for Mommy," Kerri said. Taking a small bunch of flowers to leave at the headstone had been one of their rituals.

"Well, we'll make sure we have time to buy one next visit," Quincee promised, turning down the road that would take them to their destination. "But you know, I'm sure they have fields and bushes just full of flowers with lovely smells in Heaven. What do you think?"

"Uh-huh," Kerri replied. "My Bible school teacher says God made all the flowers and trees. I bet Mommy loves having flowers all around. She likes roses best."

"Then I just know she can have roses anytime she wants them," Quincee replied.

When they reached the cemetery Quincee allowed the children to race down the aisle of the grass-carpeted enclosed field while she followed at a slower pace. Nothing had changed since their last visit to the small familiar headstone over a month ago; the cemetery staff kept the park-like setting in perfect order. The children tenderly greeted their mother and offered a few bits of information about yesterday's yard sale. But Quincee's heart eased when they didn't seem to feel the heavy grief they once did.

Then they surprised Quincee by being ready to leave much sooner than expected, and Quincee drove home in thoughtful wonder. Perhaps they were all experiencing a readiness to move on with their lives, she mused, and the recent enforced absence from that part of their lives had helped them all to refocus.

Thank you, Lord. We'll never stop loving or missing Paula, but it does help to know she's happy and with You....

Quincee pulled into her drive and parked right in front of the garage. She did, indeed, need to refocus her summer efforts. She really had to finish cleaning out her garage. Now that she could drive again, she had a ton of errands to do; she'd add a trip to the dump to her list, taking whatever she couldn't use or sell.

"I'm hungry," Kyle complained as he scrambled out of the car.

"Again?" Quincee teased, closing her car door. She swiped a tissue across her dewy upper lip, as the idea of a tall glass of iced tea tickled her fancy. "You're a bottomless pit, d'you know that?"

"Can I have a snack?" he asked.

"You can have some fruit for now, but—" Kyle raced away, and Quincee laughed. She glanced at Kerri, who had slipped her hand into Quincee's. She hoped the kids would be happy with grilled cheese sandwiches for supper. "Are you hungry, too, Kerri bear?"

Kerri nodded, yet Quincee thought the child was more tired than hungry. Kerri didn't take well to late nights, and the last two had been very late for the children.

"Quincee! Kerri!"

Kyle's call held urgent excitement. Quincee's heart jerked in automatic fright, and she dropped Kerri's hand to sprint ahead. As she rounded the corner of the house, the fleeting worry of what now tumbled through her head. She caught Kyle as he flew into her.

"What is it?" she asked, holding his arm as he struggled to free himself. She rapidly searched the boy. No bleeding or broken bones in sight. She let her heartbeat slow down.

His eyes the size of teacups, Kyle tugged at her, pointing. He held his breath, a look of sheer reverence on his face. "Come see, Quincee. Kerri, hurry!"

She raised her gaze. There beside the front steps stood two shiny new bicycles, one red, one blue. One a boy's, one a girl's. The red one larger, the blue a size smaller with training wheels.

A safety helmet hung from the handlebars of each cycle. One red. One blue. And elbow and knee pads.

"What?" Quincee murmured under her breath. "Kyle, don't—"

Kyle, already running a loving hand over the handlebars, shouted, "It's okay, Quincee. They're ours. Mine and Kerri's."

"Kyle, wait a minute," she cautioned as he slipped the helmet over his head and kicked the stand to fold away. "We don't know whose these are yet. It may be a mistake."

"Uh-uh," he said, dragging out the sound. "I know. See? There's a tag with my name on it."

Kyle was off before Quincee could stop him.

As Kerri inspected the blue bike, Quincee checked the tag on it. Sure enough, Kerri's name was typewritten there, but with no sign of who the giver might be.

"But it isn't Christmas," Kerri said in wonder as she checked out the training wheels on hers.

"No, it isn't Christmas," Quincee murmured. Who would be so generous? Who knew that Kyle wanted a bike more than anything? Who knew them well enough to know she couldn't afford to buy the children bicycles right at this time?

The Longacres? They were lovely people, but they had their own grandchildren to provide for. Randolf? No… Although he'd been more than generous in his way, she couldn't picture the gruff old man buying the children expensive gifts. Besides, none of them really knew just how tight her circumstances were.

Hamilton knew….

The children's excited voices sounded musical in the quiet afternoon. Quincee caught her breath.

Hamilton knew.

She slowly turned and stared across the two yards that divided her house from Hamilton's. Letting her gaze rove from his backyard to his glorious wraparound front porch, she spied his tall figure stretched out on a lounge chair there, a place he seldom occupied. He appeared to be absorbed in the newspaper.

He'd been waiting for them.

"Kerri," she said in her well-modulated, no-

nonsense voice she used in the classroom "you may ride along the sidewalk between our house and Hamilton's until further notice. Put your helmet on, please."

She craned her neck to call the boy, who was circling back to them. "Kyle, you may not ride in the street unless I'm out here to watch you. You may ride…um…" She assessed the distance swiftly before laying down her rule. "Down as far as the Tillotsons' house, but not farther. Do you both understand?"

"Yes." The answer floated over Kyle's shoulder as he wheeled off. Quincee could only shake her head in amazement. Where and when had the boy learned to ride?

"Will you help me, Quincee?" Kerri begged.

"Sure, honey," she answered, keeping her gaze on Hamilton. He hadn't moved an inch or turned their way by a flicker of an eyelash. That newspaper must hold a fascinating article, she mused. Gripping, in fact.

"But in a few minutes. Right now I have something to talk to Hamilton about. You stay here, all right?"

Quincee didn't hurry, but she strode with resolve as she marched up the sidewalk, turned at his walk and climbed his front steps. She stopped a yard in front of him, her fist on her thrust-out hip, her lips pursed.

She said nothing for a long moment, simply brushed the hair from her forehead.

He glanced at her over the top of his paper. His eyes gleamed with laughter, the gray softening into silver. "Do you want something Quincee?"

Laughter! From Hamilton Adam Paxton III?

"You!"

"You want me?" He raised quizzical brows, amusement threatening to spill out like a waterfall.

"That's not what I meant, and you know it."

"Then you don't want me?" The corner of his mouth quirked. "I kind of thought you did. What a pity."

She ignored that while she shifted, tapping one foot. "It was you who left those bikes for the kids."

"Bikes? What are you talking about?"

"Don't play innocent, Hamilton." Flinging out a hand, she pointed right at him. "You, of all people in this Harry Truman town, can't get away with it. It's completely out of your character."

"So?"

"I want to—"

"Don't." His smile faded a little.

"Don't what?"

"Say it. Not a word." His caution rumbled out in his judge's tone. His eyes said something else.

She sighed, losing her dogged stance. "But you can't just give my children expensive presents, Hamilton."

"I'm over twenty-one, Quincee." His paper rattled as he folded it carefully and lay it beside him. Then he slowly rose to face her. "I can do whatever I want to as long as it's not illegal or immoral. Does giving the children a gift fall under either of those categories?''

"No, of course not. But it simply isn't..."

"Isn't what? Aren't the sizes right? Don't the children like the colors I chose?"

"You know very well the children are over the moon with delight." She let her hands fall to her sides, complaining, "I'll never get them to bed tonight."

"Then what's your objection? Do you want to rob me of my pleasure?"

Quincee paused for a long moment. Finally, staring at the narrow boards in the porch floor, she mumbled, "It feels too much like charity."

"It's not meant that way, Quincee," he said very softly. "It's merely a gift to two young friends whom I've grown to like very much. Don't let your pride get in your way, or let it deny the children something so important to them."

"It isn't something they need. They don't need everything they want...."

"I don't disagree with that, Quincee, but in our culture, children need a few harmless things to give them equality with their peers. It brings them happiness and builds self-confidence."

Behind them, the whir of wheels called their attention to Kerri, even with the front porch. Quincee could barely breathe. The bike teetered, but remained upright with the training wheels.

"Look, Hap. I can ride my bike just like I said," Kerri called.

"That's terrific, Kerri. You are a true athlete," Hamilton called.

"See, Quincee? I can go fast."

"Yeah, you sure can, Kerri bear. But not too fast, please, until you get used to it," she begged.

Hamilton slipped his hands in his pockets and returned his gaze to Quincee. "You see? Already Kerri has more self-confidence. Now tell me you haven't done, or given, to some of your students with the same thought in mind? You can't, can you? It's in my means to easily provide a couple of bikes for Kyle and Kerri, so why not?"

Quincee leaned on the railing. "All right, Hamilton. You win this round, and the children will heap blessings on you forever. But I want to... What can I do for you in return? You know, I'm very good with wallpaper. If you like, I'll not only do your parlor over, I'll take on your dining room, too. And those drapes really need to go, just like the ones in your den. And although I haven't seen your upper floor, I'll warrant—"

"Hold up there, Wonder Woman." He lifted a hand and chuckled outright.

She loved the sound of his chuckle. She could spend years listening to it and never tire of hearing it. He exhibited it far too seldom.

She'd have to think of other things to make him laugh.

"You don't have to exchange anything for my goodwill," he continued, almost too solemn. "You don't have to barter, pay back or otherwise owe me. A thank-you will be quite sufficient.''

Quincee tipped her head and narrowed her eyes, her heart picking up its beat for the umpteeth time today. Only this time for a far different reason than fear or sorrow. She let a smile curve suggestively. ''A thank-you?''

''Ah…a verbal expression, please. Not a demonstration. The neighbors are watching.''

''You didn't like my demonstration of thanks yesterday?''

He cleared his throat. ''I don't like public displays that lead to… They often lead to other people jumping to the wrong conclusions.''

''Okay, so I embarrassed you. But did you like my thank-you?''

His ears tinged to red. ''It wasn't necessary.''

''Did you?''

''Yes!'' His gritted glare made her chuckle.

''That's all I wanted to know, Hap.'' Quincee felt smug and couldn't keep it from showing. ''Now I'll send the children over to say their thank-yous.''

The little tease! Hamilton watched her swing away and skip down the front porch steps through narrowed eyes. Her walk was saucy, her swing pert. He knew she knew—he was watching every curve of her body as she took herself home. But he couldn't take his gaze anywhere but her sassy figure.

''Want to go to a parade on Tuesday?'' he called.

''You know where there's a parade?'' She paused to ask, half turning.

"Sure do." He stepped down one step. "Later we can take the kids out to Fort Osage or Missouri Town and watch the fireworks."

"All right."

"I'll pick you up at eight sharp so that we'll have plenty of time to get a good place to view."

"We'll be ready." She took two steps backward. "Shall I pack a picnic?"

Though his body urged him forward, he rooted his feet to the bottom step. This was as far as he went.

"That would be nice."

"It's a date!"

From the corner of his eye, he saw movement on the Longacres' lawn, a flutter of Bette's print skirt. He turned and hurried up his steps.

Chapter Thirteen

Fourth of July wore all the bright, sparkling attributes of a long, perfect holiday.

When the sun shone hot, the trees offered shade. The activities at Missouri Town proved fun and fascinating for all of them, and Hamilton bought small American flags for the children at the gift shop. They found a great spot by Lake Jacomo to eat their fried chicken and potato salad and watched the sailboats while they munched. They ran a few races between them, played with a Frisbee and rested under the trees. Then the evening filled up with wonder, oohs and ahs when the fireworks filled the dark sky.

More than once throughout the day, Quincee wanted to pinch herself. Surely this absolutely lovely day was a dream; it was entirely too idyllic.

As they drove home with the kids asleep in the back seat of Hamilton's sedan, she found herself silently praying.

Oh, Lord, please let me keep the memory of this day without anything spoiling it. There's been so many blessings of late, I'm almost scared to ask for anything more. But this is what I want for my life...a full family set, and a place of my own to keep in peaceful harmony.

Was that too much to ask for?

This last year, too many days had been fraught with problems and concerns, she realized, and quickly added, *Father, thank you for a day of release from care. Only You could have known how much we all needed it.*

Hamilton carried Kerri into the house and into the bedroom without hesitation while quietly directing Kyle to find his own bed. Then, laying Kerri on her bed, he glanced over his shoulder at Quincee, eyes twinkling. "This is beginning to feel as though I'm in training for something."

"Oh?" she whispered, raising a brow in teasing curiosity. She moved forward to remove Kerri's shoes and socks, then gently tucked her under the sheet. Sleeping in their shorts and T-shirts wouldn't hurt the kids for one night, she decided. "What would that be, do you suppose? Assignment to family court?"

Hamilton leaned against the door frame and watched her. "Family law...I'm not sure I'd ever properly qualify for that."

His tone grew serious, and she straightened. Something troubled him at times, she noticed. Yet he'd softened toward her and the children so much that she knew he found real pleasure in their company.

And in hers, she hoped.

Why was he still single, anyway? Usually all the good men were taken by the time they reached their thirties. Didn't the man want to marry? Have children?

Bette had told her he'd gone through several girlfriends in high school and a half serious relationship in college, dating a girl for whom his grandfather had high hopes. Nothing had come of it.

Quincee led the way out of the house, peeking into Kyle's room long enough to be sure he'd kicked off his shoes. Outside, she paused on the stoop.

Across the way, a back room night-light shone from the Longacres' house; Quincee thought they'd gone to spend the holiday with one of their children. Randolf Bader had lights turned on in his living room, and she suspected he was, as usual, watching television to fill his lonely hours. A bit of guilt waved through her for not inviting him to spend his day with them; she'd invite him to dinner soon.

Down at the far corner, a car turned into the street and parked in front of a house whose occupants she had yet to meet. Up and down the street, many of the houses were dark. The air smelled of sulphur and lingering smoke, evidence that someone in the neighborhood had set off fireworks.

The moist night air had cooled only by fractions, but it wasn't unpleasant. Hamilton didn't seem in a rush to go home, so she sank down on the top step and patted the cement beside her. "It's been a lovely day. Sit awhile, Hamilton."

"All right," he murmured, his tone deeper than the night. He rested his elbows on his knees, his fingers laced, and gazed silently at the street.

Quincee breathed deeply and let out a slow breath. Today had been a marvelous, special day plucked out of ordinary time, leaving her feeling content and hopeful for what her future held. Something very like happiness filled her horizon, but she shied away from looking at it too closely in fear of it all shattering into bits. Peace seemed the best attribute of all, at this moment.

Lord, I could use more of this... I surely could.

"Now tell me why you say that family law isn't for you?" she asked.

Hamilton glanced at her in surprise. Hadn't he expected her to pursue the subject?

"Oh...I think my views are often too rigid to show much compassion for family problems. According to a couple of my colleagues, sometimes they're downright jaundiced."

"Hamilton, I can't imagine you giving out any judgment that would go against the laws of balance and rational thinking. How could that make you rigid?"

"There are some who would disagree with your assessment of me. Even you thought me too harsh in the, ah, circumstances of our meeting."

"Well, I, um, I didn't think you *awfully* unfair..."

"Mmm?" His challenge left her no room to wiggle. "You didn't?"

"Okay, maybe a little. But that doesn't count for anything. Now continue, please." Hamilton seldom confided his inner doubts and emotions, and she wanted to keep it rolling. "About why you think you couldn't be a good family court judge."

Hamilton shifted to lean his chin into his palm, his elbow propped on his knee, and let out a sound between a grunt and a sigh.

"Judges who deal with families need the wisdom of Solomon. As you know, within reason, a judge has certain leeways within the judicial framework. But I can't…don't…give away much even when it's in my power to be lenient. Very few times have I even wanted to offer a lighter penalty for an offense. I've always felt that most people won't get it unless they face a stiff consequence for whatever actions have brought them into court."

"Yes, I've noticed that," she said, her tone dry.

"Uh…" He slanted her a glance, then grimaced. "Yeah, well…you are no exception, young woman."

"No, you're right," she agreed with one of her saucy grins. "Absolutely. You can't make exceptions for anyone or the law wouldn't work. Unless there are extreme extenuating circumstances. I didn't really expect any favors."

"Okay, now that we have that out of the way, you can tell me why you got those parking violations and speeding tickets."

Quincee sighed and shoved her hair away from her forehead. She needed to get it trimmed, it was always in her eyes these days. "Oh, you don't want to hear all that. It's over now, and I've lived through the aftermath."

"I'd like to hear it, Quincee."

She shook her head. "Not really, Hamilton."

He made a half turn her way, his brows lowered. "Don't presume to read my mind for me."

"All right, all right," she said with a half smile and a long, indulgent sigh. She rubbed her knees, listening to the occasional sound of distant traffic, and tried to order her thoughts of the last year. The last chaotic six months.

"Well, my sister Paula was ill...."

She bit her lip to keep it from trembling. Now would not be a good time to cry, Quincee admonished herself. The judge must've seen too many women in tears from the bench. Besides, she'd done all her crying.

"And one of her last requests was to eat at a popular restaurant. So we took the kids and went. I didn't have a handicapped permit, but I knew she couldn't walk far and needed my help, as well." She shrugged. "So I took a chance and parked in a space reserved for those with a card. It just so happened it was a bad choice on a bad day. Someone got angry and complained. Then another time, I parked in a no-parking zone on the street because—well, some of the same reasons. But—" she rushed to finish "—I confess to speeding a couple of times when I shouldn't have. That's it.''

Hamilton listened without interruption, his gaze never leaving her face. She averted her eyes after speaking—to cover her tears, he suspected—and stared into the street.

The Longacres came home, Gene parking their small car so that Bette could get out at their walk. The elderly couple didn't seem to notice them, intent on taking themselves off to bed, he supposed.

There was a lot Quincee hadn't said. Details of how she'd coped between long days of teaching and her responsibilities for her sister's care and the children's. He didn't find it hard to imagine how frazzled she may have felt on those occasions when she got those driving points. A floodgate inside him lifted, and compassion flowed through his veins like a river. She'd carried quite a load, he thought, and heaven only knew how she'd accomplished her balancing act.

His instinct was to take her into his arms. To share her grief and soothe her hurt.

He didn't dare. He might not stop with mere comfort. There'd already been a dozen times today when he'd yearned to kiss her, opportunities he'd ruthlessly shoved aside for a swift meeting of lips, implying promises he had no business in even thinking.

But it was getting harder.

After the Longacres closed the door behind themselves, he spoke, letting his compassion fill his tones.

"Quincee, why didn't you seek help? There are organizations and people who would've given you some."

"My friend Laura did help," she replied quietly. "And some of the other teachers. They covered for me when I had to leave early or go in late. They brought Christmas dinner and bought the children clothes and gifts. They were real angels. And Laura went to bat for me on the house loan, too, and helped me move. Other things…"

"You've learned to barter for."

"That's it. Besides, I've adopted Philippians Four, Thirteen as my motto. You know—I can do all things through Christ…"

"Who strengthens me." Hamilton joined her on the last phrase, then responded with a grin when she chuckled. "Yes, it seems to me I've heard you recite it once or twice. And you often practice Proverbs Seventeen, Twenty-two, as well," he continued. "A joyful heart is good medicine."

That was Quincee, he realized. She went about doing things with a joyful heart. Without self-pity. Her penchant for bartering sometimes sent him into an irritated tizzy, but he had to admire her tenacity. She'd set quite a course for herself.

"Ah…" She leaned back on her hands and tipped her head at him. "That's just self-defense. Comes naturally to a bubbleheaded woman."

"Don't put yourself down, Quincee."

"I won't if you won't," she quipped.

"What do you mean by that?"

"Tell me again why you don't want to be a family court judge?" she asked.

"On that, I think it's time to go home," he said and rose. And on that, he suddenly gave in to the all-day temptation he'd struggled so hard to resist.

He brushed his long fingers against her soft cheek, tipped her chin up and kissed her. A soft, velvety kiss, gentle and restrained, but barely holding back the river of heated passion that rushed between them.

Quincee made a tiny little sound deep in her throat, and he pulled her closer, anchoring her small body against his. His fingers dropped to her throat. He caressed the delicate skin, stroking even lower, over her collar bone where it met the rounded neckline of her cotton blouse.

He wanted her to invite him into her small, cramped, impossible house. Impossible because the children were there and there was no room, no privacy. Then he wanted to pick her up and carry her into his house, to carry her upstairs to his bed, to shut the door, shut out the world and be just the two of them. To just be...

Someone two streets over set off a string of rocket bombs. The snap of explosions pierced the quiet, jerking them both out of their daze. Inside the circle of his arms, Quincee jumped. Hamilton dropped his hands and stepped away, breathing hard.

Quincee felt like she'd run a three-minute mile. She struggled to slow her air intake.

"That's someone's last hurrah, most likely," she said, her voice strained.

"Yes, I suppose it is," he said, his tones hitting what sounded like the canyon floor. "Well, I have to be in a meeting by eight in the morning, so I'll say good night."

"Good night," she whispered. Quincee couldn't move.

He got in his car and turned on the motor. She watched him as he backed out of her drive and drove the few yards to turn into his own. His car disappeared from her view on the far side of his house.

The spell broke, and she slowly went into her house. But not to sleep. She lay for a long time, listening to Kerri breathe, staring out her window, angling her body so that she could see the outlines of Hamilton's bedroom window.

Lord, I wonder if Hap would let me decorate his bedroom....

Chapter Fourteen

Climbing to the highest point on the ladder, well anchored, Quincee slowly began painting the front of her house. The thirsty boards soaked up the primer, and she wondered if she'd have to use three coats of paint rather than two. She'd chosen pure white and planned to accent it with a deep blue trim. Below her, the children rode their bikes furiously, making the first run of the morning over their allowed territory.

Hamilton backed his car out of his drive, waved to the children and was out of sight in moments.

She sighed. He hadn't looked her way. Of course, he wouldn't expect to see her out already this morning. It wasn't yet eight. But he'd barely waved at any of them for a couple of days, and she wondered if she'd done or said something to put him off.

Funny. She hadn't realized she'd miss his company so much. Did he miss hers even a little?

Other neighbor worker bees left for daily destinations. She counted eight cars passing within the hour, almost emptying the street. Gene greeted the children when he came out to pick up his Kansas City *Star* and the Independence *Examiner*. Gene liked to be well-informed, she'd noticed. Unlike Randolf, who could care less if he kept up with national news as long as he could hear the local happenings on television and had someone with whom to share the neighborhood gossip. He came along about ten to say hello and hand out advice.

"You know what you're doin' there, Quincee?"

"I'm learning as I go, Mr. Bader. The best teacher is experience."

"You have ta be careful on those ladders, y'know." He gave a hitch to his baggy shorts. "We had a fella from where I worked one time who fell off a ladder and broke his leg in three places. He like to never got that leg healed."

"My ladder is very secure, Mr. Bader." She continued to ply her brush. "But thanks for your concern."

"When're you going to come get that piano?"

"Well, that does take some thinking about, now, doesn't it? I wonder what professional movers charge?"

"No need to pay big money to have that thing moved only two doors away. It's just an old 'un. We can rent one of them dollies and do it ourselves."

"That's an idea, all right, but I'm not sure if either of us have the muscles to lift it on and off the dolly."

"Get them Rodriguez boys to come and help. They do bodybuilding."

"I just might, at that," she answered, continuing to ply her paintbrush. She'd met the Rodriguez youths during the yard sale. But she couldn't think of a thing with which to barter a work trade. She'd have to offer them a fee.

"Hey, Kyle, watch it. There's cars using the street this time of day," Randolf Bader said by way of greeting the next morning. He chatted to Quincee's back for about thirty minutes as she steadily worked her way around the small house, telling her all the neighborhood news.

"And ol' Gene's been wondering how long before you 'n' Hamilton'll be moving in together."

"What?" She twisted on her ladder so sharply, she banged her shin. She grabbed for the rung just behind her as she stared at Randolf. "Why would you think Hap and I...that is, Hamilton and I are only friends."

"I didn't say such a thing," Gene said as he strolled up behind Randolf. "You're putting words in where you shouldn't, old man."

"You said they were gettin' mighty close, you can't deny that!"

Quincee backed down one ladder rung, her brush held aloft. A spatter of paint hit her cheek, but she paid no mind. "Now, gentlemen, I think we need to get something straightened out. I am not—"

"Bader, you need to watch your mouth." The two men faced each other, Gene waving his folded paper, his reading glasses falling to the end of his nose. "Getting close is one thing, but what you accuse me of saying is a sight more serious."

"People do it all the time these days," Randolf said loudly, his nose growing red as he sidetracked the point. "Live together. Don't mean nothing anymore."

"We are not living together," Quincee insisted.

"It would mean something to Hamilton," Gene retorted, nearly shouting, shaking his paper in Randolf's face. "He's a judge, and a fine man to boot. He watches his good name, he does. Like his granddad. And it matters to Quincee, too, I'll warrant."

Kyle wheeled into the yard and stopped, straddling his bike as he observed the grown-ups, his gaze flying from one to another. Kerri paused on the sidewalk, her gaze puzzled and frightened as she inched closer to her brother.

That's all she needed, Quincee thought. To cause the children any more upset for whatever reason.

"Guys—" She held fast to the ladder, fumbling above her but failing to find a place to lay the brush down. Finally, she stepped to the ground.

"Judge or not, Hamilton's another generation than his grandpa," Randolf grumped. "These young people don't see things the way we do, you know."

"Um, guys, please..." Quincee laid a gentle hand on Gene's arm, wondering if she'd have to physically separate them as she did scruffy boys during school hours. Perhaps she should send Kyle for Bette.

"I heard my name mentioned," Hamilton said,

suddenly among them. His sober stare didn't invite a friendly offer of morning coffee. "Is this another neighborhood meeting I should attend?"

"Hamilton! I thought you'd gone to work already," she squeaked out, almost strangling on her words. What had he overheard?

"Forgot some papers." Hamilton frowned, studying the two older men, then making a swift examination of her face. "You fellows have nothing better to do today, the meals on wheels program could use some help."

Quincee bit her lip in embarrassment.

Randolf hitched up his shorts and ambled away. "Well, I got, uh, washing up to do."

"I think m'wife's calling me," Gene mumbled. He turned on his heel and hurried across the street.

Quincee wanted to explain that... Say she'd had nothing to do with...

It hadn't been her fault.

It didn't matter. The neighborhood gossip had a life of its own, and it had already reached mountainous proportions, she suspected. Sighing, she said nothing while she gazed at the paintbrush, turning it over in her hand. Finally, she glanced at him.

Hamilton stared at her for quite half a minute, then stalked away, saying, "I'm late."

He wasn't an easy man to read, she mused, but she knew he wouldn't like being the center of gossip. In fact, he'd hate it. He wasn't one to indulge in idle talk on any subject. How much would he blame her for the current chatter, she wondered?

Suddenly she had no audience at all. Time to get on with her work, she mused. Then by way of distracting the kids, she offered, "Do you two want to help paint?"

"Yeah!" Kyle's face brightened, a grin hovering around the edges of his mouth. He rolled his bike to stand by the front steps. Kerri copied her brother.

Quincee found her bucket of supplies and pulled out two small brushes. She gave the children a space against the lower wall and showed them how to ply their brushes. Then she climbed her ladder, mulling over what she should do about this latest knot in her life.

Except...

All at once, she paused, staring at the patterns in the boards that cried out for paint, realizing she wouldn't mind at all if the gossip were true. Nothing about his occasional gruff moods put her off. She imagined a dozen ways of teasing him out of them.

What if she and Hamilton could end every evening with the kind of sizzling, sweeter-than-sugar kisses they'd shared the other night? Every night spent together...

But for her, the fantasy of living together began with marriage.

And she didn't think Hamilton was the marrying kind.

It took Quincee two full days to apply the primer—which seemed easy after spending so much time scraping off the old paint and sanding all the rough spots. She was left to work in peace—no one came by to caution or advise again.

She felt pleasantly tired on Friday night, and after putting the kids to bed for the evening, she soaked in the old tub for a long while.

She put on a sleeveless cotton nightgown, made herself a tall glass of iced tea and then sat down at the small dining table to tackle her bills. She'd delayed paying many of them until the last possible moment before a penalty would apply.

Afterward, she threaded her fingers through her hair, counting her totals for the third time. Her bank balance looked anemic, but she felt good about seeing her outstanding debt slowly diminish. She'd run her credit high during her sister's illness and in buying the house.

The bonus of the block sale had been a boon, but she couldn't count on unexpected events to bail her out every month.

She sipped her tea as she contemplated her finances. The next year or two would be tight, no lie. And again this month, her small amount of remaining cash had to stretch tighter than Grandma's girdle until month's end, so they'd be eating more spaghetti and hot dogs.

If she must, she'd take a Saturday job, but she wasn't there yet.

Lord, so far You've provided for us beyond my hope. Thank You, and again I'm trusting You to see us through. Just save us from any more emergencies like Kerri's illness. Please? I do praise You for her quick recovery.

Yes, the Lord had blessed them.

And Hamilton had given Kerri two lovely tomatoes from his garden. They'd been a wonderful addition to supper. He'd given them some early peaches, too.

She hadn't seen or spoken to Hamilton since the fracas with old Randolf and Gene. Come to think of it, she hadn't seen anyone at all but the children since then.

The evening was still warm. She brushed her hair from her nape, allowing the air to cool her skin. Only ten—she didn't feel sleepy yet. Packing away her shoe box of monthly bills, she pulled a paperback novel from her stack of reading material and curled up in the corner of her couch to read for the rest of her evening.

She dozed and awoke some time later.

Outside, the street was quiet. She rose and strolled to the screen door, listening. Most of the houses were dark. From somewhere came the faint delicate strains of a waltz. She opened the door and leaned out to try pinpointing the source.

She caught a breath in surprise. It came from next door! A light shone from Hamilton's library, and she wondered what kept him awake.

Since when did Hamilton enjoy waltzes? She stored away her new fact and made a quick decision. She dressed, then checked all the locks, made certain the children's windows were left open so she could hear if they called and let herself out of the house.

There she paused. At one time, she'd think nothing of visiting a friend in the middle of the night, but now... She reminded herself that she didn't run in a careless single crowd anymore; she had children in her care. She couldn't leave them alone even to run next door. It didn't feel right.

But she needed some adult conversation. She wanted that conversation to be with Hamilton.

She'd have to settle for a phone call.

Taking her cell phone, she settled once more in the corner of her couch.

"Hello." He answered on the second ring. Just hearing his deep tones gave her shivers. It felt like eons since she'd spoken with him.

"Hi, Hamilton..."

"Quincee?"

"Yes."

"Is something wrong?"

"No."

"Then why have you called?" Impatience laced his voice. "Do you know what time it is?"

"Um. About midnight, I guess. Does that matter? You're awake. I'm awake. I saw your light and thought..."

"Thought what?"

He didn't want to talk to her. She'd intruded on his space.

"Nothing..." She sucked at her bottom lip, trying to push the disappointment away. "I suppose I just wanted a little company. Sorry to have bothered you.''

"Quincee, don't!" He sighed, then ordered, "Meet me by the back hedge."

He didn't wait for an answer, assuming she knew the exact spot. And she did. The children's arch, the growing door between her yard and his.

Fingers of light from the street lamp made shadow patterns across the grounds. She picked her way along the hedge until she found the arch. He was there almost as soon as she, and ducked to come through.

"This isn't wise," he murmured, pausing in the shadows. "Old man Clarke who lives behind you is a light sleeper. If he doesn't take us for trespassing and call the police, he could shoot us for burglars."

Quincee giggled, covering her mouth for fear of the sound carrying in the night. "You're teasing."

Hamilton didn't tease. Never. She thought it delightful.

"Not by much," he responded, a gentle laugh threading his voice. He took her elbow and guided her to the old bench. "Old Clarke did let off a shotgun blast late one night a couple of years back. Scared the stuffing out of the woman walking her dog."

"Has that happened often?"

"No." They sat on the bench, only inches between them. "Clarke's daughter took the shotgun away from him. But he does phone the police on occasion."

"Well, let him complain. There's no law against paying a call on a friend, no matter what the time."

He let that go, reaching out to brush the feathery curls from her face. His touch was sure and sweet. "Why aren't you sleeping?"

"Couldn't." She held still, loving his touch. "Why aren't you?"

He dropped his hand, and she yearned to grab it back. She searched his dark profile for a hint of what he may be thinking, listening to the nuances in his tones.

"I'm wrapping up something I'm doing for a friend."

"Has it been a lot of work?"

"As a matter of fact, it has. But I haven't minded. Until lately, my work was the most important thing in my life."

"Until lately? What's changed?"

"I'm not sure exactly...." He stared toward the top of his house.

"Oh." Disappointment threaded her soft utterance. She'd hoped he'd think she had made a difference in his life. A good one, rather than merely an annoyance.

"But—" he leaned an inch her way "—I have a strong suspicion it has to do with my...altered needs."

"Ah, yes." Her heart lifted, and she turned her body toward his. "Nothing ever remains the same in life, does it?"

"Would you want it to? Remain static?" His breath fell softly on her cheek.

"Oh, I don't know." She lifted her mouth, silently inviting him to reach for her. "I've had a lot of change to deal with this last year, much of it—"

He brushed a finger across her bottom lip.

"—difficult. Any new change would have to be one of colossal—"

His thumb stroked just under the line of her jaw, sending shivery notice down her body.

"—earth-shattering value to get my total attention."

"Ah, yes," he murmured, nuzzling her ear, sliding his arm around her. "That's it. I'm finding my attention totally engaged in a new, earth-shattering direction."

His mouth found hers, and Quincee nearly groaned with pleasure. His lips held a piercing need, and she urgently wanted to satisfy it, to fulfill her own.

She felt a major loss when he withdrew, gulping air. Leaning against him, her breath came in shallow gasps.

"Mmm…this isn't…a bit wise," he muttered, kissing her again, short, sweet little nibbles against her mouth.

"No…"

"One more."

"Only one?"

"Only one more for now…"

The kiss almost melted her down to a puddle at

his feet. He broke away as though he were breaking chains of steel, finally gently pushing her from him.

"Come on, I'll walk you to your door."

He held her arm, strolling to her back door, touching the tip of her nose before saying "Go to bed, Quincee."

Resolutely, he pushed her inside.

The next day, Hamilton took an unusual call from his pastor, William Tate. Pastor Tate rarely called him during professional hours.

"Hello, Bill," Hamilton said, leaning back in his black executive chair. He'd just returned from lunch and had about five minutes before returning to the bench. "What's up? Has the parking lot committee run into a problem in expanding our space?"

"Ah, no, Hamilton," Bill Tate replied awkwardly. "It's, ah, a little more personal than that. The thing is, I got a phone call from someone who lives in back of you. Uh…"

"Old man Clarke."

"Yeah, that's the name."

"What is he complaining about now?"

Bill cleared his throat. "Hamilton, maybe you could come by for a chat soon. I, ah…"

"Just say it, Bill. What is Mr. Clarke's complaint?"

"He is accusing you, a deacon of our church, of unholy visitation with your neighbor, Miss Davis."

"He what!"

"That's his expression, not mine. He claims to

have witnessed you and Miss Davis engaging in a 'hotter than Hades X-rated embrace as you came out of her house' and if I don't chastise you he's going to give the whole sordid story to the *Examiner*. What's this all about, Hamilton?''

Hamilton let out a sigh, not knowing whether to laugh or take the old man's threat seriously. Yet, the scripture said to avoid even the appearances of evil.

''Oh, you know how it is, Bill. People in public office are subject to all kinds of character attacks. But I'll admit he did see me kiss Quincee Davis. We were saying good-night in her backyard. However, I can assure you that… Oh, blast, Bill. I can't tell you exactly what's happening between Quincee and me, but I haven't acted improperly or done anything to embarrass my position as deacon.''

''That's all I wanted to hear, Hamilton,'' Bill said. ''We'll lay these rumors aside. If it comes up again, I'll let you know.''

''Thanks, Bill. You're a brick.''

Breaking the phone connection, Hamilton shook his head in disgust. Some people delighted in making mischief. His clerk knocked on his door, telling him it was time to return to the court. He'd have to think about this problem later.

Chapter Fifteen

❧

Late on Saturday afternoon, Quincee came down from her ladder to see a black truck drive slowly down the block, then turn around at the corner, cruise back and park in front of her house. Two people sat and stared at the house a moment, then at her.

A man got out of the truck and advanced toward her. Her heart began to slam against her chest.

His mop of dark blond hair stuck out from beneath a dirty ball cap. His bronze skin contrasted with his hair, attesting to his outdoor work. But his features strongly resembled Kyle's. And Kerri's.

It had been years since she'd seen the children's father. Five, to be exact. Shortly after Kerri was born. How had he located them? How, after all this time, had his company finally located him?

What did he want?

Her gaze darted to Kerri, parked with her bike in

front of Hamilton's house waiting for him to come home. To Kyle, racing his bike toward her at rocket speed, already curious as to who their visitor could be.

Instinctively, she wanted to scream for the kids to come to her, to hide them behind her like a mother hen or rush them to safety as though threatened by a tornado.

"You must be Quincee." Mac Stillman spoke with a jovial tone. "Remember me? Long time no see, ain't it?"

No words immediately came to her. She simply gaped.

Why now? What did he want?

A dragon tattoo snaked up Mac Stillman's forearm. His fingernails were grimed with dirt. His wrinkled short-sleeve shirt hung open over a white sleeveless T, and his jeans sported holes at the knees. In spite of all that, his even white teeth flashed in a smile that was quite charming.

Quincee licked her lips and found her voice. "Yes, I remember you. You've been a hard man to locate, Mac."

"Yeah, guess so." He stuck his hands into his back pockets, his quick smile changing just as swiftly to a doleful moue. "Sorry about Paula. Wish I coulda helped, but—" He shrugged, suggesting helplessness.

Anger burned a heavy path through her mind. Was he, indeed? Then why hadn't he stayed in contact with her sister? Why hadn't he made the effort to see his children? To see to their welfare?

"When did you get my letter about Paula's illness?"

"Uh, back a time, I guess. When my mail finally caught up with me."

"Why didn't we hear from you?" She failed to contain the ire that edged her voice, and didn't care.

"Couldn't do nothin', now, could I? I didn't have no money to come then," he said, whiny enough to cause her to grind her teeth. "And you said it was hopeless."

"Didn't you get an urgent message from your company to at least call me? A phone message or an e-mail?"

From the corner of her eye, Quincee noted Kerri leaving her post. She pedaled furiously over the short distance toward home.

Mac shifted from one foot to the other. "When would that be?"

Calmly, calmly, she admonished herself. Attacking Mac wouldn't resolve a thing.

But Lord, I'd sure like to wring this insensitive jerk's irresponsible neck! He doesn't care a fig about how Paula suffered, how much Paula once loved him or how she worried about their children's future.

Then it hit her. If Mac Stillman didn't care enough to answer Paula's need for help or to pay child support these last five years, then why had he come now?

How had he found her and the children?

Quincee carefully stuck the paintbrush in a can of cleaner and grabbed a rag to wipe her hands. She didn't look at him. "Not long after Christmas."

"Nope, don't remember that. But I was kinda wiped at Christmas and hung over in January." He turned to the woman in the truck. "We didn't get no message from Weaver sometime in January, did we, Debbie babe?"

"Not that I recall." The woman, dark-eyed and with bright, well applied makeup, slid out of the truck and sashayed into the yard. Her tight jeans showed every movement of her generous curves.

She smiled broadly and introduced herself. "Hi, there. I'm Debbie Crane."

"Hello." Quincee responded in casual fashion as Kerri came up and edged to her side. Staying calm for the children was a primary goal, she reminded herself.

Kyle arrived, skidding to a stop in front of the steps, where he parked his bike. He sidled up to stand beside her, staring suspiciously at the two visitors. Kerri half hid behind Quincee.

"I bet you're Kyle," Mac said with a wide grin.

"Yeah," Kyle challenged. "Who're you?"

"Why, I'm your daddy, son. Mac Stillman." He leaned sideways and reached out as though to chuck Kerri under the chin. "And this can't be my baby girl?"

Kerri jerked away, burying her face against Quincee's back, her hand clutching Quincee's belt loop.

"My daddy doesn't live around here," Kyle challenged through squinting eyes.

"That's right, son, I don't. Sorry I haven't come to see you much. Traveling with my job keeps me tied up, see. But I'm your dad, sure enough. All you have to do is look in a mirror to tell it."

He turned to his girlfriend. "Don't they look just like me, babe?"

"Sure enough do, honey pie," Debbie crooned. "You surely did put your stamp on them."

"You're not *my* daddy," Kerri suddenly spoke.

"Yes, I am," Mac answered in surprise.

"Uh-uh." Kerri shook her head, her under lip stuck out in defiance. She pointed to Hamilton's large Victorian. "My daddy lives over there."

Quincee held her breath. She'd known that Kerri had attached herself to Hamilton, but nothing had prepared her for how deeply it had gone. Or how much Kerri needed a father. Or how horrible this meeting would be.

Stupid, stupid!

Somehow she'd been caught completely unaware, and she shouldn't have. Just because Mac Stillman had ignored Paula and the children all these years brought no guarantees he wouldn't make a claim when it suited him.

Mac couldn't really want the children, could he? He never had before.

He bent over to speak to Kerri. "I don't think so, little girl. I think I'm your daddy. And I'm here to get acquainted with my kids. Who lives over there, anyway?''

Kerri, her mouth quivering, retreated behind Quincee again. Automatically, Quincee reached out a protective hand, gathering the child against her body, brushing the petal-soft cheek under her fingers.

Father, I need Your strength and wisdom right this moment. Please, Lord...tell me what to do, what to say and how to handle this situation without anger. If he's here to take the children...

No one bothered to answer Mac's question, and after a moment, he addressed Kyle. "You sure are tall for a six-year-old."

"I'm seven." Kyle's frown rode low on his forehead.

"Uh, no lie? Seven?" Mac's grin flashed. "Well, well, time sure does get away from a working man. Deb, here, is always tellin' me to pay attention to things, especially after my third beer."

"That's right, sugar. You don't remember your own name after a Friday night paycheck party." Debbie brushed her long dark hair over her shoulder and chuckled. "But I made him save enough money to come see y'all this time. We drove eighteen hours to get here, but I told Mac that a man's gotta go see his children once in a while."

"That's right. Just had to come see my two kids." He glanced at Kyle, his mouth going doleful. "Now that your mama's dead, I guess I have to take care of you two."

"What do you mean by that?" Quincee asked, her heart beating fast. "Kyle and Kerri are in my care."

"And you've been mighty kind to watch out for 'em, too, little sister." Mac swept his cap from his head and wiped the sweat from his brow with a forearm. "Say, you wouldn't have a cold one in your fridge, would ya?"

With the movement of muscle and bone, the dragon wiggled along his skin, and behind her, Quincee felt Kerri's clutch on her leg tighten.

Calmly…calmly… Find out what he wants.

"No, sorry. I can offer you some iced tea."

"That'd be real nice, hon," Debbie replied. "We didn't stop for lunch."

"We should all go in, I suppose," Quincee agreed, struggling to keep the reluctance out of her voice. "We have—"

She'd started to say they had a lot to discuss, but she suddenly didn't want to put words or ideas into play before she found out what Mac really wanted. She hoped it truly was only a visit.

"We ate lunch from a leftover noodle casserole. There's some left, if you're hungry."

"Um, none for me, thanks." Mac swiftly covered a distasteful grimace. "But I will take that tea, if you don't mind."

"Sure," Quincee replied and led them into her living room.

Leaving them there, Quincee hurried to the kitchen. Kyle stayed behind, never removing his suspicious stare from his father, but Kerri followed Quincee, stepping on her heels in her anxiety.

"Kerri, pour some lemonade for you and Kyle," she suggested, giving the child a reason to be with her as well as keeping Kerri occupied.

Quincee brought out her best cheap glasses—she'd never had money enough to indulge in good china or glassware—and searched her bottom crisper for the mint leaves Bette had given her only this morning. Delaying tactics, she knew. She didn't give a rap if Mac and his girlfriend were impressed or not, but she needed the time to calm down and think.

No one, up until now, had questioned her right to keep the children. She had Paula's notarized statement naming her as guardian and her formal letter requesting Quincee raise them. That had been enough for the last six months.

Would that stand in a court of law? She'd have to ask Hamilton. He'd know, or direct her to someone who did.

She wished he was home. She prayed he'd return home early, but she had no idea where he'd gone today.

She decorated a tray with a cloth napkin, added three glasses of iced tea with mint leaves and carried all into the living room. Mac and Debbie occupied the couch, so she sat down in the side chair. Kyle stood guard, leaning a shoulder against the wall beside the front door.

"I only take orders from my immediate boss," Mac was telling Kyle. "I don't have much truck with the high ups. Been moving around a lot on the job. Never stay no place longer than a couple a weeks or so.''

So why now? The question repeated itself all through Quincee's thoughts like an echoing drum. Why, after all this time, had Mac Stillman come to see his children?

"Thank you, hon," Debbie murmured, reaching for a glass of tea. "Sure is hot today. Didn't know Missouri got this steamy."

Mac tipped his glass and drank. "Yeah, I told Debbie it'd be hot, but she didn't believe me. That's 'cause she thinks Missouri is way up north."

He laughed, enjoying his joke.

"Don't you have no air condition?" Debbie asked, glancing curiously around the small living room while she lifted the rounded neckline of her cotton shirt away from her body. She held her cold glass against her throat for a moment.

"Our window unit has gone on the blink," Quincee answered. She felt sticky all over, too, and heartily wished for a cooling bath. "We're saving for a new one."

"Well, when we get a new motor home, we'll have all the comforts," Mac said. "You kids will like that, won't you?"

"And generally, we can park in a campground that has a pool and a playground," Debbie added.

Quincee's heart plummeted at the implications, but before she could say anything, ask what Mac intended, Debbie burst out.

"Oh, hon. We left the presents in the truck. Go get 'em, Mac."

"Yeah, that's right," Mac said. "We didn't want to come with empty hands, now, did we?"

The screen door slapped behind him as he left. Kyle watched from the doorway.

"Can I refill your tea?" Quincee asked, proud of her apparent cool control when she wanted to explode.

"Thanks, think I will," Debbie replied.

This time Debbie followed Quincee and Kerri to the kitchen. Kerri edged herself to Quincee's far side, her distrust of the stranger painfully obvious.

Quincee added ice cubes to Debbie's glass and poured the last of the tea.

"Can I use your can?" Debbie asked, looking around curiously. "Been drinking too many colas, y'know?"

"Yes, of course," Quincee answered. "Through there."

"Quincee, when is my Hap coming home?" Kerri whispered plaintively as soon as Debbie was out of sight.

The anxiety and fear in the child's bright blue eyes yanked at Quincee's heartstrings.

"I don't know, Kerri bear." She squatted on her heels to hug the child. "Hamilton had business to take care of today. But I'm sure he'll be home soon."

Mac should have warned them he intended to make a visit. Why now, when she and the children had all settled into living together in their new neighborhood? They'd grown comfortable and gained a bit of peace.

This visit shouldn't have happened without preparation. Kerri didn't understand the situation and neither did Kyle. They were frightened with the sudden appearance of a father they didn't know. They didn't know what to expect, and neither did she.

Quincee automatically began to wash the paint stains still marking her wrists, thinking of her paint drying in the heat, of the tools that needed putting away, wondering... Worrying...

I'm frightened, too, Heavenly Father. I don't know what to do...or what will happen if Mac Stillman demands custody of his children. A father does have the right to raise his own children, but Kerri and Kyle belong with me. It was what Paula wanted. Mac hasn't shown any interest in them until now.

But he was here. Today.

Do not be anxious about anything.... The clear thought ran though Quincee's mind as Debbie returned to the kitchen. *In everything, by prayer and petition, with thanksgiving, present your requests to God.*

It was the passage from Philippians her adult Bible study class had used last week, a part of the same chapter where her motto was found. She'd hungrily absorbed it, not realizing how soon she'd need to hear those very words again. Or put them into practice. *Do not be anxious about anything....*

Jesus had taught trust, total and complete trust in

Him. For salvation, for the way of life, for victory over adversity.

Father, I want what's best for the children. Help me. I think they're better off with me, but I'll trust You to direct this thorny path...and thank You for hearing my heart.

"You have only two bedrooms here?" Debbie asked, startling Quincee from her silent prayer.

"Yes," she answered with a gulp. "Just two."

"Too bad..." Debbie gathered her hair over one shoulder and asked, "Don't suppose you have a hair band by chance? I gotta get this hair up."

"Uh, no. Sorry."

"I'd have thought you'd a gone for something much bigger with a couple of kids. More roomy and modern, a town house, maybe."

Quincee didn't know how to answer, so she made no attempt to do so. Had Mac and his girlfriend hoped to stay with her as guests?

"Kerri, sugar, come on in here and see what your daddy brought you," Mac called from the front room. "Got a bee-u-ti-ful doll here that's got your name on it."

Debbie reached for her tea. "Yeah, Kerri, we brought you a gorgeous— Where'd the kid go?"

Quincee glanced about the kitchen. The child wasn't there.

Chapter Sixteen

"Aren't you worried about where the kid has got to?" Debbie asked, glancing around. She seemed to assess the contents of Quincee's kitchen with one quick sweep, and by the swift twist of her mouth denounced it as wanting.

"Um, not really," Quincee murmured. "She's gone next door to look for her friend Hamilton. She adores him."

Kerri had run to where she felt safe. Most likely, she was curled up on Hamilton's front porch wicker chair. Quincee wouldn't mind running to find Hamilton, either. Hamilton could tell her what her rights were about keeping the children; he'd know what to do, who to call on a Saturday night for legal advice.

"I never knew a kid who didn't want a present," Debbie complained, heading into the living room. "Well, I suppose we can leave her doll here for now."

Quincee followed, wanting to push these people out of her house and send them home.

Kyle fingered a baseball mitt, turning it around as he inspected its construction. By his expression, he didn't know how to react, but he didn't show the wild enthusiasm he had when he'd received his bike.

"Did you remember to tell your dad thanks?" Quincee prompted.

"Thank you," Kyle said, in a noncommittal fashion.

"You're welcome, son," Mac replied, nodding in satisfaction. "Knew a boy would want a ball mitt."

"I'm worn to a frazzle, Mac," Debbie insisted. "Let's go find a motel and get some Zs."

"Yeah, fine. Suppose we should." Mac turned toward the door. "Gotta talk, though, Quincee. Get our arrangements straightened out. Gotta get back to work by Tuesday morning, so we'll have ta pack the kids up tomorrow by noon, the latest."

"Pack up the children?" Her heart slammed into her ribs. Her hope that this was merely a visit drained away. He was serious.

She hadn't really believed it until this moment, and her thoughts tumbled out before she thought. "What are you talking about? They live here with me."

"Now that's the thing, Quincee. I appreciate what you've done for 'em, taking care of them for Paula, but I'm their daddy."

Quincee began to shake with panic.

"Mac, let's talk about this," she said, fighting a

rush of tears. "Please? You can't just arrive and take the children out of the blue like that. This is their home. They won't understand."

"What's to understand? I can't waste time from work, now, Quincee. It won't do no good to argue."

"But Mac, they hardly know you. Give them some time. You're a stranger to them. Up until now we didn't even know if you were alive or dead, never mind where to find you. You said yourself you move around all the time. How can you take care of them? They have to go to school...."

"Yeah, yeah, I know all about that." His mouth twisted in distaste. "That judge hammered me about my responsibilities. He wouldn't let up till I said I understood. Sent a cop out to talk to me, even."

"What judge?"

"The one that called me. Talk about the long reach of the law, that was stretchin' his stuff, if you ask me. Callin' the cops on me for nothin' but doin' what God made men for. Getting myself a couple of kids ain't no crime." He shook his head in disgust. "But old Paxon, Paxley, whatever his name was, said he'd get me for non child support if I didn't pay attention. Have me thrown in jail."

"Judge Paxton?" Quincee felt like someone had hit her in the head with a brick. She rubbed her palm against her temple, trying to dispel her stunned feeling. "Judge Paxton called you?"

"Yeah, that's the one. Wonder who sicced him onto me?"

That's what she'd like to know...who. What had she told Hamilton?

"What did he say?" A sense of betrayal churned Quincee's stomach. She wanted to weep. She wanted to slap him silly. How could he? How could Hamilton do this to her? To the children?

"He made threats, that's what he did." Mac's face flared with hot resentment. "Hung up on him the first time. I thought he was a bill collector. But Deb, here, talked to him the second time. She made me see that it might not be so bad to take the kids with us, especially with another income an' all."

Quincee flashed a glance at Debbie, who was idly twisting her hair into a knot. Helpless rage flared again, and Quincee felt...less than charitable.

Lord, help me. I don't normally feel this outrage when something goes against me.

Why would Debbie want the children? She hadn't struck Quincee as the mothering type.

Quincee swallowed hard and pushed down her wild irritation. She struggled to make her tone reasonable. A frontal attack wasn't the right approach; she could only hope a reasonable one would work.

She cleared her throat. "Mac, you can't seriously want the children to live with you. Think about it. Young children are a lot of work. Every day. Think of all the responsibility you'll have."

"Don't you worry, now, hon," Debbie said, crooning sympathy. "We plan to take care of the kids just fine. Specially when we get a new rig.

That'll set us up good. They'll have their own bedroom and everything.''

It was more than Quincee could provide. "But what about school?"

"Deb'll teach 'em," Mac pronounced. "That's how other families on the move do it. We'll manage, won't we, Deb?"

"When I have to, I will," Debbie said, shrugging. "Didn't like school when I was a kid, so I don't much cotton to the idea of teaching. But with regular money coming in, maybe we can pay for a real teacher now and again. 'Sides, TV has lessons these days."

In Quincee's experience, the image Debbie painted came across as a minefield for child neglect. She'd taught students who had little or no supervision at home, and her heart always cried out in protest. Some of those situations degenerated into outright child abuse.

No! She couldn't let that happen to Kyle and Kerri.

"Mac," she said, ruthlessly smothering all pride to beg. "Don't do it this way. Please. Um...come back for supper. Let's talk about it. You need to talk to Kyle and Kerri more. Find out how they feel."

"Uh, don't know about that..." Mac hedged. "It's Saturday night. Wasting a good Saturday night is a jail offense, for real. Thought I might look up a couple of my old haunts as long as I'm here. Debbie's quite a looker when she's all dressed up."

"Sure, we'll do that," Debbie said, addressing

Quincee as she nudged Mac. "Now, Mac. Think about what Quincee is saying. We don't want to travel with a couple of screaming kids all the way back home with you hungover, now do we?"

Mac considered that a moment, glancing at Kyle. The boy stared with a belligerent expression so tight, Quincee thought he might explode. She wondered where he'd found his toughness. The baseball mitt lay on the floor, carelessly dropped.

In answer, Mac's mouth tightened. "Nah, guess not. But you ain't gonna do that, are you, Kyle?"

The implied threat settled over them like dust.

"Nope," Kyle declared, his jaw firm. "I won't. 'Cause I'm not going at all. I'm staying with Quincee."

Quincee held her breath. Obviously, Kyle had taken a distinctive dislike to his father, but to defy a grown-up outright wasn't like the boy.

"Your aunt don't have nothing to say about it," Mac snarled. "I'm your daddy. If I say so, you'll come with me."

"Mom said me 'n' Kerri would live with Quincee. I'm staying here."

Quincee laid a calming hand on Kyle's shoulder. "Mac, let's talk about this later. You and Debbie are both tired. So am I, really. It'll be easier after we've all rested. We, um, all need to get used to this idea."

Some of Mac's aggressiveness abated, but the glint in his eyes remained hard. "Okay. But I warn you. Don't you pull any…stuff on me, understand?"

Quincee bit her lip. What kind of stuff? Did he think she'd pick up and run away, like he had?

"Come at six," she said quietly.

Like a soldier sentinel, Kyle watched from the window as Mac and Debbie climbed into their truck and drove away. Then he whirled on Quincee, his hands curled into fists.

"You won't make me go, will you, Quincee?"

"Kyle, tiger..."

"You can't. I don't like him. Don't like her, either."

"But he is your dad." Quincee's heart felt shredded. She couldn't deny her dislike for Mac, but if she voiced it, let her feelings show, it would pile more hardships onto the kids if they were forced to live with Mac.

"I don't care. I don't remember him. And Mom didn't like him anymore or she would've told me. He didn't love us, ever."

"You don't know that, Kyle." Perhaps it was true. Maybe Mac did love them in his way. "He simply hasn't been around to show his love."

"No, he doesn't," Kyle insisted, his tone fierce, his eyes dark with pain. "If he did, he'd a come when Mom was sick. Before she died. And I'm not going with him."

Quincee turned her head to hide the tears rolling down her cheeks. Kyle's truth twisted a knifelike wound into her heart. Not because she disbelieved or disagreed with his statement, but because the raw, ugly knowledge came out of a boy who hadn't yet reached his eighth birthday.

"Kyle…" She let a long, shaky breath out of her lungs, her shoulders slumping. It shouldn't be that a child of such tender years knew such adult pain. And she'd failed to shield Kyle from it.

Lord, help me…. The desperate cry rushed through her spirit as never before. *Help me protect these precious little ones from harm of any kind.*

"Let me go collect Kerri," she murmured, giving Kyle a swift hug. "And then we can decide what to serve for dinner."

"When is Hap coming home?" Kyle asked. "I'll bet *he'll* think of something to help us."

Quincee's vision clouded with a hazy red. Hamilton? Oh, yes, that self-righteous priggish judge had thought of something, all right. The two-faced joker. He just couldn't resist stirring up her life, whether it made sense of anything or not!

She left her house and she almost ran up the sidewalk. As she'd suspected, Kerri sat on the front steps of the wide porch.

She'd just reached Kerri when Hamilton's car pulled into his drive. Ignoring him, turning her back, Quincee scooped the little girl up, holding her close in her arms. How much longer would she have the privilege?

"Well, hi, there, girls. Are you waiting for me?"

Beyond the pleased, measured tone, Quincee heard the car door slam shut. *I'd like to slam more than a door right now.* Her thoughts whirled. *I'd like to find*

*someplace to take the kids and barricade us against
all outsiders. Including this one. Maybe then we can
live without interference.*

"I was just thinking about a tall cool soda," he
said. "Want to join me?"

"Hap!" Kerri squealed, and squirmed to get
down.

Quincee tightened her grasp and started down the
steps without looking his way.

"Quincee, I want my Hap," Kerri wailed.

She ignored the child's plea.

"What's wrong, Quincee?" he suddenly demanded.

She said nothing and kept walking.

"Quincee?" His hand clamped around her shoulder, hauling her to a stop at the end of his walk.
"What is it? Where's Kyle?"

Quincee jerked away and spun on her heel. She
glared her wrath, wishing with all her might that she
was taller so she could go nose to nose with him.

"I—you—" She clamped her mouth tight on the
bitter accusations she wanted to hurl at him.

"All right. I see you have something about to
blow." He calmly set his briefcase down on the cement and began removing his tie. "Spit it out."

"I'd love to, thank you very much! Don't you
move a muscle, Judge Paxton," she commanded
through gritted teeth, shaking her finger. "I have a
lot to say to you. Oh, do I ever! Stay right where
you are."

On stiffened legs, she marched a few yards down

the sidewalk and set Kerri down, saying, "Kerri bear, run along home for a few minutes. Tell Kyle to get into the tub and clean up. I'll be there in just a few minutes."

Staring over her shoulder, for all the world looking deprived of her most precious treasure, Kerri dragged herself home.

It didn't make anything easier. If her anger wasn't so well rooted, Quincee would've chuckled over Kerri's woebegone little face. But her heart ached too hard for laughter to relieve anything this time. If Mac Stillman made good his claim, little Kerri would indeed be deprived of her beloved Hap's company. Perhaps forever.

And would she ever see the children again?

Lord, if that should happen, I'd never regain a merry heart. It would be broken into a thousand pieces.

Then she realized. Hamilton had already punctured a thousand holes into it. But while her love for him melted with the flaming hurt he'd thrown her way, she'd hang on to her anger. It may be the only thing she had left.

She marched to Hamilton, her voice rising higher with each step. "You double dealing, underhanded skunk! How could you? Why?"

Hamilton paused in the act of folding his coat. He raised a brow. "To what are you referring?"

"Sending for Mac Stillman."

"Oh?" One foot on the first porch step, he rested

his jacket on his thigh while he rolled up his shirt sleeves. "So he made contact, did he?"

How could the man be so calm? Didn't he know what he'd done?

"He made contact, all right. He's here in town, big as you please, with no thought of preparing the children for his return to their lives."

"That's good."

"Good?" She stepped up one step, satisfied at last to square off with Hamilton Adam Paxton III on what she thought of as equal terms. "*Good!* That is the stupidest thing I've ever known you to say. Brainless, do you hear me? How can you? How could you have sent for him?"

"Quincee, you told me you tried to find him yourself. Why are you so mad?"

"But I didn't think he'd come here. He hasn't before. I thought he'd simply ignore us and let us get on with our lives."

"Don't be simplistic, Quincee. The man needs to live up to his obligations. From what you've told me, he's gotten off scot-free of responsibilities all these years. He owes thousands in back child support. It's criminal."

"So you just had to stir things up."

"I follow what the law demands, Quincee. He's the children's father. If he doesn't want to be a father, he at least has to help financially. You need child support. You're barely making it between paychecks now."

"But we were making it! Yes, it's tight, but... Oh,

why couldn't you just let it alone? Leave us alone? Now he wants to—'' Her voice broke, and she ended in a sobbing whisper. "Take the children away from me!''

"Oh, Lord. He doesn't.'' Disbelief flitted across Hamilton's face as he pulled in his chin. "What exactly has he said?''

"What does that matter? He is the children's father and he's demanding I pack their clothes by tomorrow. How can I deny him?''

"Yet he's never shown an interest in them before?''

"No,'' she said on a sob. "I don't understand this, really. Why now?''

She sank onto the step and gulped. "I have to think of *something* between now and six. Kyle's likely to run away if I don't.''

"What's to happen at six?''

She explained her invitation and her hopes of dissuading Mac and Debbie from yanking the children from her. Then, gazing at him with her heart in her eyes, she entreated, "You're a judge. Can't you stop him? Have him arrested and thrown in jail for…for neglect or at least—''

"I've told you before, Quincee,'' he said. "I won't use my position for personal favors of that nature. But if I talk to Stillman, then perhaps we can better assess the situation and find a solution that satisfies you both.''

"You've already done enough talking, Judge Paxton.'' She gritted the words out. ''Whatever you said before was what brought him here.''

''Nevertheless, count on one more for dinner.''

''Fine.'' She rose and jabbed her finger into his chest. ''You do that. You come. You come and enjoy dinner with that louse who thinks a high sperm count and a five-minute bit of fun is all he needs to make him a father. Because it may just be the last time you see any of the rest of us.''

Hamilton wrapped his long fingers around her small hand, enclosing her pointing finger, holding it tight. ''Now, Quincee, calm down. Don't do anything rash.''

''Calm down? Is that all you can say? Calm down? That hasn't helped me so far.''

She jerked her hand free and stomped off. ''And the only rash thing I've done these last two months is fall hysterically, unaccountably in love with a stiff-necked judicial type who is all square corners. And if I have to give up Kyle and Kerri, it definitely will be the last time I ever speak to you.''

Chapter Seventeen

By six sharp, Quincee had prepared the meal and set the table. She'd bathed and dressed in a blue princess-cut print dress with matching high-heeled sandals—an outfit she thought of as last year's dating attire.

She made sure that the children looked their best, too. If this turned out to be a farewell dinner, then by golly, she'd do a grade-A job of it. She'd secretly let her tears roll while bathing, but ruthlessly harnessed all her fears the moment she came out of the bathroom.

She'd remain calm if it killed her, she'd decided. The children would never see how scared she felt of losing them. Or just plain scared....

I can do all things—it seemed to Quincee those words echoed in her mind every five minutes without conscious effort—*through Christ Who strengthens me.*

A plan hadn't occurred to her yet, if the worst happened. If she couldn't talk Mac out of demanding immediate custody of the children. But she still pinned her hopes on making him see reason.

"You look very pretty, Quincee," Hamilton said when he arrived promptly. He handed her three red tomatoes and a box of chocolates. "For the table and after."

Quincee accepted his gifts and tipped her head at him. The gifts sidetracked her harried thoughts long enough for her to realize this was the first time he had ever complimented her on her looks. What was he up to? Or was this his way of making a peace offering?

Actually, in spite of the unhappiness in her eyes, Hamilton thought her the prettiest thing in his life. Ever. He'd never seen that exact shade of blue on her, and realized it matched her eyes. With her strawberry hair fluffed around her face, she looked alive and vital.

She made *him* feel alive and vital, and all this past week he'd been envisioning what it would be like to have Quincee as his wife, filling his life with excitement and joy.

If he could stand never knowing what she might do.

Now, seeing her dressed up in something that flattered her petite figure instead of the usual loose T-shirts she wore, he realized that having her on his arm at the few professional social functions he attended would make him very proud. Heavens, he didn't care what she wore—she appealed to him in every way.

Then, as she turned away, he let a smile hover around his mouth. Inviting Quincee Davis into his often stuffy circles might prove very entertaining, as well. If the current situation weren't so serious, he'd sweep her up and kiss her soundly. Spontaneity could be learned, after all.

But the anxiety Hamilton saw in Quincee's eyes sobered him. He yearned to gather her in his arms and tell her all would be well. He couldn't say that yet.

However, he had a plan. If it worked, if Mac Stillman was the kind of man Hamilton thought him... But he had to play the wait-and-see game. There were too many unknown variables.

Kerri rushed out of her bedroom and flung herself at his legs. Her blond hair stood out from her head in two floppy dog ears, tied up with pink ribbons to match her clean pink shorts outfit. "Hap. I've been waiting and waiting forever."

"Hi, there, Kerri bear." He swung the child up. "I think I've been waiting and waiting, too. But here I am at last. Do I get a hug tonight?"

Kerri hugged him tight, her little arms circling his neck, and Hamilton thought the all-powerful feeling of love that welled up in his chest must be the most precious gift God had ever given him.

Father, is this how You love Your son? Can this amazing love I feel for these children even touch a tenth of how much You love each of us—to count us also as Your children? If my plan works, Father, let me be worthy…. Ah, God, yes, let me be worthy.

"Where's Kyle?" Hamilton asked, setting Kerri on her feet.

"He won't come out of his room," Quincee said, her eyes showing a well of misery. "I didn't see any reason to make him until necessary."

"May I talk to him?"

"Yes, of course." She glanced at her watch. "Mac isn't here yet."

A few minutes later, Kyle and Hamilton came into the kitchen asking what they might do to help. A smile played around Hamiton's mouth, and when Quincee glanced at Kyle, she saw another. What had they talked about, she wondered?

She let it go. *Whatever it is, Lord, if it helps Kyle…*

Debbie and Mac arrived thirty minutes later in the middle of a quarrel. Debbie wore a blouse that hung low on smooth white shoulders and a denim skirt that barely reached her thighs.

"For goodness sake, Mac, but I had to get something to put my hair up off my neck, didn't I?"

Debbie smoothed her hair where it was caught up with a red scarf to cascade over one shoulder.

"You didn't need that new top!"

"Well, cookie, you didn't seem to mind waiting in that bar down the street. You could've done without that third beer."

"So what's your point? After all your bit—um, uh, fussin' to find a mall and whining about the heat,

I had to have some relief,'' he answered on a sour note. ''Now shut up about it.''

Quincee opened the door for them, and Mac broke out his charming grin. ''Hiya, kids. Here's your old pa again, just like I promised. Are you getting your stuff packed?''

''Now don't you look just like two angels,'' Debbie crooned in spite of the children drawing back. ''Don't they, Mac?''

''Yeah, I guess they do,'' Mac replied, losing interest as he spotted Hamilton. His gaze grew suspicious.

Quincee made swift introductions.

''Hamilton…'' Mac gaped, his eyes bugging out. ''Hamilton? That's— You're him! That blasted crazy judge that tracked me down.''

''I am.''

''What the all-fired—what's going on here? Why're you here?''

''Hamilton is here for dinner, the same as you,'' Quincee said firmly, working on her calm acquirement. ''And since it's been ready for a while, please come into the dining room and let's begin.''

Mac hesitated, his stare belligerent. ''What are you trying to pull here, Quincee? Are you setting me up for something? I don't see a need to call out a judge.''

From the corner of her eye, Quincee noticed Debbie smoothing her short skirt as she cast a flirting gaze Hamilton's way.

''Hamilton is a good friend, Mac,'' Quincee said

without a flicker of an eyelash. "Like you and Debbie are friends. We often enjoy a meal together."

"Oh, I getcha, Quincee. So that's it."

"Ooh, you have interesting tastes, Quincee." Debbie displayed her overbite for Hamilton. "From what Mac said, I didn't think your notions went in that direction."

"Well, guess you've grown up some, at that." Mac spoke with a leer, running a lustful gaze down Quincee's small, feminine body.

Hamilton threw her a cautioning glare.

Quincee silently ground her teeth, but bit her tongue on the scathing vocal hits she wanted to sling at him. At Mac and Debbie, too.

Lord, don't You think calmness can be overrated?

"Can I sit by Hap?" Kerri asked, her gaze entreating.

"Hamilton is to sit at the head of the table for tonight, Kerri." Quincee beseeched Hamilton with a glance, and he gave her a quick nod. "But you may sit at his right hand, and Miss Debbie may sit on his left. Kyle, will you help me bring the food in from the kitchen?"

And a minute later...

"Hamilton, will you ask God's blessing?" Quincee asked on a quiet formal note when everyone was seated.

Quiet and formal. Calm qualities she'd cling to for now. She couldn't allow herself to think too far ahead.

"Surely." Hamilton bowed his head. He paused

to allow Debbie's rustling to cease. "Father, we thank You for Your provision in all things, in all matters, at all times...but in particular now for this dinner. And we ask a special blessing for the gracious one who prepared it. In Jesus's name, Amen."

Hamilton's low voice sounded a deeper timbre as he spoke of her to God, even in that generalized way. It sent waves of warming love over Quincee, and hope for what may come of this evening. Silently, she added her own words of thanks. *Jesus, thank You for being the bread of life. I give over all my fears to You. Thank You for sending Hamilton to help me.*

Help her?

Where in the world had that idea come from, Quincee questioned. She was still steaming at Hamilton for finding Mac Stillman, for bringing that lazy do-nothing into their lives—never mind that she'd tried to inform the man. What's more, she'd be raging like a mother lion if she couldn't sidetrack Mac from stealing the children from her.

If she could only convince herself that Mac really cared for Kyle and Kerri... *Oh, Lord, I'll be heartbroken if I have to let them go...but if their father truly cares for them, at least I wouldn't fear for their welfare.*

For the first few minutes, conversation came in awkward clumps as bowls of vegetables and the meat loaf were passed around. Quincee kept her eyes lowered for a long moment, searching for a way to lead into a discussion of the matter on all their minds. Her thoughts centered on laying out a plan for a gradual turning over of custody if Mac couldn't be persuaded to leave the kids with her. It would give her time, give them all time. What else could she do, besides persuade, explain the children's need to remain with her…and beg?

Practice trust in God, and composure, she admonished herself. Finally, she drew a deep breath and asked, "So, Debbie, how did you and Mac meet?"

"Oh, we met in a little town east of Augusta when Mac's crew was there last summer. Went there looking for fresh territory, if you know what I mean." Debbie giggled and stirred more sugar into her tea.

"After three months of putting up with the local bar rats—" Debbie rolled her eyes at Hamilton "—I didn't have no trouble saying yes when Mac invited me to join him, you can believe it."

"Ah… And what do you do? I mean…" Quincee passed a basket of bread and searched for a diplomatic way of asking before she continued. "Nine to five?"

"Oh, this and that, I guess. Mostly hairdressing. I like to do people's hair." Debbie paused, waving her fork in the air toward Quincee. "Now, hon, you could tone down that red and go truly blond with no trouble at all. You'd look real cool as a blonde."

"Thanks for the suggestion," Quincee answered. She glanced at Hamilton, noting with sudden amusement the don't-you-dare glint in his eye. "Maybe later in the year when the new school term begins."

"That's right. You're a teacher, huh?"

"Yes. I teach fifth and sixth graders."

"Quincee always was a sucker for kids," Mac said fondly.

Quincee nearly snorted with disgust. Mac had never shown her a fondness in his life. In fact, when he and Paula were together, Quincee and Mac had sniped at each other on a regular basis. Except for the time when she baked his favorite cake to please Paula.

Well, she wasn't sorry to have missed that opportunity. She was counting on mere cookies for dessert today.

"That would drive me to tequila sunrises, for sure," Debbie said in awe. "They couldn't pay me enough to teach for real. I don't really cotton to watching out for a whole passel a brats."

"Oh, that age can be energetic, I admit. But I don't think of them as brats," Quincee answered, questioning how long it would take for Debbie to think of Kyle and Kerri as brats. "They're fun and challenging."

"I'll be in third grade next year," Kyle pronounced, adding stubbornly, "at my new school, only three blocks away."

"Nah, you're joshin' me," Mac said, ignoring Kyle's reference to the school. "Third grade. And what grade will you be in, Miss Kerri?"

Kerri shrank back in her chair and shifted her gaze helplessly toward Hamilton.

"Kerri will begin kindergarten in the fall," Hamilton supplied. "Quincee has already registered the children in the new school."

"Kindergarten is just baby stuff," Kyle said.

"I'm not a baby," Kerri declared. "Am I, Hap?"

"No, of course you're not," Hamilton reassured her. "Your brother merely likes to tease you, so pay him no mind."

"Well, it won't matter," Mac said with a shrug. "You'll be together in home school anyway."

Kyle scowled. Kerri simply looked puzzled.

"Third grade is a crucial, foundational year," Quincee murmured. She stared at her plate, the food barely touched. If Debbie were to teach them, what if Kyle missed too much of his academic basics? How could the boy move forward?

"There are some excellent home school programs on the market now. Which of them do you favor, Miss Crane?" Hamilton asked.

"Oh, um, whichever one Mac likes, I guess."

"I'll have to look into it," Mac responded. "But babe, we gotta get ourselves set up better first."

He turned to Hamilton. "See, up till now I've been pretty footloose, makin' do with a twenty-foot old tin bucket and sometimes motels an' such."

"I'm sure that made it difficult for you to stay in touch with the children," Hamilton said, his tone dry. "Hard to get to a telephone or mailbox."

"That's right," Mac said, ignoring the censure. "Always on the move. But a couple of my crew buddies have newer trailers they haul from town to town, and one of them even takes his wife and kids. They do real good. So Deb an' I looked at a thirty-footer before we hauled ourselves up here, somethin' we can drag easy enough and still give us room for the kids.''

From her deepest center, Quincee pulled a long, shaky breath. "Children, you may be excused now to go ride your bikes."

"Really?" Kyle scooted out of his chair and was gone like a flash. Kerri moved slower, with one lingering stare over her shoulder.

Kerri hadn't eaten much of her supper, but Quincee couldn't bring herself to make a fuss. Even Kyle hadn't indulged his usual starving appetite.

"So," Quincee said as soon as the children were out of earshot, "you haven't bought your trailer yet?"

"Nope. That's something we've gotta talk about, Quincee, girl. I'll need the insurance money Paula had," Mac stated. "That should be enough to pay for most of the rig."

"What insurance money is that?" Quincee gave up trying to eat and leaned back in her chair.

"Now don't give me that garbage." Mac leaned forward. "Paula had a good office assistant's job. That company had benefits. I know Paula had an insurance policy. My name was on it. I'll need you to turn that over to me."

"Mac, Paula was sick a long time. She didn't leave any money. And your name wasn't on any policy at all. Besides, the small amount of insurance she carried paid only for her medical care and funeral."

"But she worked almost eight years for that company." Mac shoved back his chair to stand, nearly tipping it over. "You can't tell me she didn't have money coming. I'm still her husband. We never divorced."

"That's not what you told me," Debbie said on a gasp, her face turning dark with anger.

"It don't matter anymore, does it?" Mac ignored Debbie and kept pressing Quincee. "What about Paula's retirement fund? Did you spend that, too?"

"Paula took care of her own funds, Mac. I didn't have it to spend. There was little enough to live on." From the corner of her eye, Quincee noticed Hamilton rising, and Debbie. Where were they all going? She wanted to cry out a protest, a panicky feeling of abandonment flowing over her. "This last year, I moved in with her so we combined our efforts."

"I don't get it." Debbie looked from Mac to Quincee. "You mean there's no money?"

"What did you do with it all?" Mac hounded her, leaning over Quincee. "Buy this falling down junky house?"

"No, I—" Trying to stand, Quincee had trouble getting her chair to move. Her stomach churning, she fought Mac's intimidation with all her strength.

"Well, you'll just have to sell it. Or borrow what you owe me, you hear?"

"That's enough, Mr. Stillman." Hamilton spoke in his canyonlike tones, his brows knit in a heavy frown. He gently pulled out her chair, which allowed Quincee to rise.

"You mean there's no money coming at all?" Debbie said on a gasp. She moved to lay a pressing hand on Mac's shoulder. "Cookie, you promised...."

"Well, you're a judge." Mac bit the words out, jerking a thumb at Quincee. "You know the law. Tell her. She can't keep money owing to me. And what about that inheritance from Paula's parents?"

"That's an educational fund, Mac. For Kyle and Kerri."

"Oh, then we have that," Debbie said with a sigh of relief. "We've got bills to pay."

Quincee stared into Debbie's pretty brown eyes and let her gaze grow harder. "No one but the children is entitled to that money. Mac can't get that money, and even the children can't have it until they're eighteen and ready for college."

"No money at all?" Debbie whined. She turned a contemptuous gaze on Mac. "You said we'd have thousands coming in between the insurance and the kids' trust fund."

Mac shoved Debbie's hand off his shoulder and growled at Quincee like a cornered rat. "You're lying, you bi—"

"That's enough, Stillman. I suggest you watch your mouth."

"I'll watch it, all right. I'll get a lawyer of my own and sue. And I'm takin' the kids tonight, ya hear? Now, right this minute."

"Mac, no. You can't." Panic gushed up to wash away all Quincee's hard-earned composure. "I won't let you."

"I'm their daddy, girl. How are you gonna stop me?"

Debbie balked. "Well, I don't want a couple of squalling kids on my hands, Mac." Her fist on her hip, Debbie stood by the door as though ready to leave. "And if there isn't any money, then why bother?"

Mac grabbed hold of Quincee's arm, his thin fingers biting into her flesh. "Quincee will cough up some money, now, won't you, girl?"

Hamilton's eyes went dark.

"It's time we took a little stroll, Mr. Stillman." His gaze was as hard as cold steel, and Hamilton's voice brooked no compromise as he peeled the man's grip away from Quincee's arm. The man had left bruises, something Hamilton would long remember. "We have something to discuss."

"I don't know what that would be," Mac fumed.

"Come along and find out," Hamilton said, propelling Stillman in front of him like a high-powered speedboat. "You might be happier if you do."

Quincee followed them out the door, Debbie dogging her heels. Across the street, Gene was watering his lawn while Bette puttered in her flower border. Randolf sat on his front porch, watching old Miss Jett.

All four heads came up as they stared from across the street. Hamilton glanced their way, then chose to walk in the opposite direction, away from them all and away from Kerri, perched on the edge of his sidewalk. Passing Kyle, he spoke to the boy, but

Quincee couldn't hear what he said. The boy headed for home.

"Now, what's going on?" Debbie asked.

"I don't know, but Hap…Hamilton has a way of taking charge of things."

"Ooh, I love a forceful man, don't you?"

"Actually, I do," Quincee admitted. A sense of pride filled her all the way to the top.

A few minutes later, Mac Stillman stormed back to his truck, ordered Debbie to get in and screeched away without speaking to either Quincee or the children.

Hamilton strolled toward her, his hands in his pockets. He never looked less like a judge; his half-smiling expression appeared more like one Kyle might wear when he thought he'd gotten away with something.

Bette glanced her way with a quick nod and a curious glance at Hamilton. Gene turned off his hose. Randolf bent over and picked up Miss Jett.

They all waited.

Chapter Eighteen

"Need any help, there, Hamilton?" Randolf gave his baggy shorts a hitch and strolled across the street, staring curiously after the departing truck.

"Thanks, Randolf, but I think I've got the matter under control." Hamilton pursed his mouth, pleased with himself.

"What did you say to him?" Quincee begged to know, wrapping her hands around her bare shoulders. She was shaking with nerves and anger and desperation. "Is he coming back tonight? Do I have to give the children over to him?"

"What? What's that you say?" Randolf demanded, his mouth dropping open.

"That's the children's father, Randolf." Of a sudden, Quincee couldn't control her tears a moment longer. One rolled down, lodging in the corner of her mouth. She licked it away. "He wants to take the children away from me."

"Never!" Randolf puffed up in outrage. "You're not gonna let that happen, are you, Hamilton? He's not taking the children?"

"Not today, he's not." Hamilton spoke decisively as he stepped to within a mere foot of Quincee's back, wanting to give her the security she desperately needed.

Desire to touch her ran through him like fire. But the need to touch her emotions, to share the urgency of his own, was even hotter.

For the moment, he had to be content to simply share information. "I—"

"Gene," Randolf interrupted to holler across the street. "Did you hear that? That bum that just left here wants to take Quincee's kids away from her."

"No!" Gene threw down his dripping hose. "You don't say. Bette!"

Bette dropped her spade and dusted her hands. Both Longacres hurried to join them.

Quincee folded her arms around herself and glanced to where the children rode their bikes. Thank goodness, they were out of earshot.

"Oh, please, Randolf. I—I shouldn't have said anything. It's just that I don't know what to do. But I don't want to upset the kids any more than they already are."

"No, of course you don't, dear," Bette said, lowering her voice to a whisper. "But what is all this now? Was that man really the children's father? I thought Hamilton was merely chasing an undesirable character away from you."

"So I was," Hamilton said. "I don't think he'll bother—"

"We'll stand with you, my dear," Bette rushed to say, patting Quincee's arm.

"Just so, Quincee," Gene agreed. "You won't have to face this alone."

"That blasted cold turkey will have to come through all of us if he tries anything," Randolf said, standing tall and hitching up his shorts with more purpose than usual. "I dare him to just try to get a piece of me."

"It won't come to that, folks," Hamilton insisted. "Besides, everything has to be done legally. By the book."

"Well," Bette said with thorough disgust. "After what you told me about that man abandoning his family and never giving your sister a dime for support, nor you, either, he has a lot to prove, if you ask me. No judge in his right mind—pardon me, Hamilton, dear—could refuse your petition to remain the children's guardian, I'm sure."

"No insult intended there, Hamilton," Gene said in an aside.

"None taken." Hamilton suppressed a grin. When he had an opening, he might tell them all that he'd already taken steps in the matter.

"I might not have that chance." Quincee could barely speak past her tear-clogged throat. She rubbed her arms, wishing for all the world that she had the nerve to step backward, to lean against Hamilton's body and draw from his warmth and strength.

"And the problems are much greater than I realized. Kerri thinks..." She paused, casting a swift glance over her shoulder at Hamilton, a fleeting wonder at the odd sparkle she saw there before continuing. "Um, Kerri doesn't believe that Mac Stillman is her father at all. She thinks her daddy is... Well, at her age she imagines... And Kyle says he absolutely won't go with Mac, and I...I can't..."

"You won't have to—" Hamilton started as he inched closer to Quincee, only to be interrupted again.

"Well, do you have a lawyer?" Bette asked. Then without waiting for an answer, she commanded, "Hamilton, dear, go call one of your friends. Right away, now. Scoot. This needs taking care of at once."

Kyle sped to a screeching stop nearby and straddled his wheels, his bright gaze whipping from one adult to another. Kerri arrived a moment later. She left her bike standing and pushed her way into the huddle, slipping one hand into Hamilton's.

Hamilton curled his hand around Kerri's tiny one and quietly spread his other palm over Quincee's shoulder. He felt her quiver and then ever so slightly lean into him.

It was all the assurance he needed. What he'd done was absolutely the right thing.

"My old law partner, John Herrick, has already been consulted, Bette. He knows family law to the letter." Hamilton's mouth curled into an impish smile. "We discussed matters at length last week."

"Oh." Bette sighed, observing Kerri's small hand in his clasp, and patted his arm. "That's good, dear. You're so like your grandfather."

"Yep, that's a fact," Gene agreed, nodding and pushing his glasses higher on his nose. "He was always on top of any given situation, too."

"We can leave it to the judge, I guess," Randolf added.

"What are you talking about?" Quincee turned to Hamilton to demand. She'd never seen Hamilton wear that self-satisfied, boyish grin before. He could well have just announced he'd won the governorship of Missouri.

"It does demand some discussion, Quincee." Hamilton tossed an apologetic glance at their friends. "A rather private one, I think. Why don't we adjourn to the front porch? That way we can keep an eye on the children while we talk."

"Ah…well, we have to get back to our yard chores," Bette pronounced. She wore her knowing smile as she headed home.

"Sure," Gene agreed, joining his wife. "Gonna be dark before you know it."

"I'm thinking I'll stroll down to the Rodriguez house and ask those iron-pumping boys if they want to earn five bucks," Randolf muttered. "Shouldn't take more'n fifteen minutes of their time to roll that piano across the street."

"That's a dandy idea, Randolf," Hamilton said. "They won't have to take it far."

"Speaking of chores, I have a half-eaten supper

and dishes to clear away," Quincee mumbled, swiping at a stray tear. She had to gain control of her emotions and figure out what to do next, and a quiet period of kitchen work would give her time to think.

"They'll wait," Hamilton insisted, taking a firm hold on her elbow, guiding her toward his front porch. "I'll help you later."

"Hap, can we see your cartoons tonight?" Kerri asked.

"Hmm...I suppose that might be arranged." In fact, he thought it a fine idea to give the children a diversion while he and Quincee...talked. "Call your brother to come home. And you must park your bike by the front steps, not on the public sidewalk to cause an obstruction."

Quincee dragged her feet as Hamilton urged her up his steps. She had no clue why Hamilton insisted on talking with her now or why he couldn't wait. He was about to burst with high spirits, while she felt weighted with misery. "Is this your way of keeping an eye on us...on me?"

"Something like that," he said, pursing his mouth.

"You think I'll run away with the kids or something, don't you? Hide out from their father."

"Would you?" He patted the cushion on his wicker love seat.

She didn't respond immediately. He gently pushed her to sit, then took his place beside her.

"Would you do that? Run with the children?"

"I don't know, Hamilton." Acutely aware of his long fingers brushing her arm along the edge of her sleeveless dress, she murmured, "I'll do what I must to protect them. At the very least, I'll follow them, make sure Mac doesn't...mistreat them or—or neglect them."

"Yes." His voice dropped to a lower register. "I suspect you'd do no less than all in your power to take care of them."

"What am I to do, Hamilton?" she cried, bringing her knees up to her chin. "Mac is gone for now, but maybe he'll come back tomorrow. Or next week. Or anytime."

"As a matter of fact, I expect him to meet me at eight tomorrow morning in my office."

"You what?" She shot up straight again, her gaze flying to search his. "He agreed to meet with you? Why? Tomorrow is Sunday. All the courts and offices are closed. What's going on?"

"A very private matter."

"A private matter that concerns the children?"

"Yes. It concerns all of us, sweetheart. You, Kyle, Kerri and me."

"I don't understand." She didn't understand at all, but she felt a sudden rush of hope. If Hamilton Adam Paxton III said he'd arranged a matter, then by gum, that was solid ground for hope.

And he'd called her sweetheart, the old-fashioned word that held more promise than a world of modern pet names.

"If it concerns me, then I should be there." Still, in spite of this new promise, her voice shook. Her entire life seemed to hang on what Hamilton said next.

"Yes, you must be there, too. The meeting will only take thirty minutes—"

Kerri ran up the porch steps and threw herself to lean against Hamilton's legs, cupping her little chin on her hands. The adoration shone from her gaze. "Hap? Can we have some ice cream?"

"Did you eat your vegetables?" he teased.

"Uh-huh."

Kyle climbed the porch steps, anxiety still lurking in the back of his eyes. He leaned against the railing and stared at his sneakers.

"Good. Good. Say, Kerri and Kyle," Hamilton said, slipping his arm around Quincee. He brushed her arm and cleared his throat. "I'd like to make a special bargain with you. You know what I mean?"

"Like when we help you in the garden and you give us strawberries and cherries and stuff?" Kyle queried.

"Yes, like that. Only this is a big, big one. Much more important."

"Okay." Kyle's gaze was riveted on Hamilton. Kerri moved to climb onto his lap, and he lifted her to sit on his knee.

"How would you like to move into this big old house and live here? All three of you?"

Quincee's breath whooshed out of her.

"Really?" Kyle's eyes widened. He lifted himself to sit on the railing, swinging his feet. "Can I learn to do that projector thing and have the cartoons?"

"Sure, I don't see why not," Hamilton nodded. "We'll discuss it. First you must learn to take care of it properly. How about you, Kerri bear?" Hamilton gazed at the child fondly. "Do you want Quincee to make one of the bedrooms all pink and white just for you?"

"Purple," Kerri said. "I want it purple."

His head tipped, Kyle narrowed his eyes and asked, "What's our job?"

"Ah, this is the serious part, and you must consider it carefully. You must agree to become my children—by adoption. I'll be your dad for all the rest of your lives. Once we do that, we can't change it. Do you want to do that? Become my son?"

"Really? Cool! Yeah!"

"See, Quincee," Kerri said in triumph. "I told you! I told you he's my daddy."

"Yes…yes, you did." Quincee's voice wobbled. For once, she didn't mind showing Hamilton a tear-filled gaze. "I, uh, I'll tell you later. And this matter tomorrow?"

"Adoption papers. Just the beginning process, but I don't think we'll have any glitches along the way. My record is public, so the investigation should run smoothly. Yours should be a simple matter with your sister's legal signature already in place for your guardianship. And, ah, we should be through in plenty of time to arrive at church for the morning worship."

Randolf strolled past them, on his side of the

street, Miss Jett on a leash. Kyle hopped off his perch on the railing. "I'm gonna go tell Mr. Bader."

The boy raced down the steps, and Kerri slid from Hamilton's knee to follow. Hamilton chuckled, the sound coming from deep inside him. "It never hurts to have neighbors you like. Especially when they know everything about you."

Quincee watched his face, watched the changing silver of his eyes, her gaze tracing the curves of his mouth as he spoke.

She loved the sound of his voice. There were still words to be uttered, and she longed to hear them.

"What did you say to Mac to change his mind about taking the children?"

"Oh, I offered a barter he couldn't refuse."

"Oh?"

"Mmm... One he seems quite happy about. I promised not to hound him about child support, future or owed, and visitation whenever he asks for it and, ah, help in attaining his...future rig, should he need it."

"You didn't offer him money?" she gasped.

"Of course not," he said with lofty disdain. "That would be illegal."

Quincee settled herself more deeply into the settee, leaning her head against Hamilton's shoulder. "And what do you see my end of this new bargain to be, Hap?"

"That's the toughest of all, Quincee," he said, nuzzling her temple. "You must agree to become my wife. My wife, my lover, my friend, my partner for the rest of our lives. And the mother of all my children. I need a full agreement between us, or you can't redecorate our bedroom.''

"Oh, that is a hard one." She lifted her chin, placing her lips within easy reach of his. His gaze held a very satisfactory glow of love. "How many children do you have?"

"Only two so far. But with God's blessing, we might fill the house." He ran a finger against her cheek, tipping her chin so that only an inch of space divided them. "Do you agree? Is it a bargain?"

"Oh, yes... You have my word, but I need one more thing to even it out."

"What's that, sweetheart?"

"The words. For a judge, you've been remarkably short on the right ones, you know."

The edges of his mouth curled with amusement while the steady gleam in his eyes held a deep, abiding tenderness.

"Aha! You drive a hard bargain, Miss Davis. But I suppose I might be persuaded. Okay, here's a first installment on a kazillion days to come. I love you. *I love you.* I love your sweetness, your never-failing courage, your determination to find the best in everyone you can. I adore your gamine face, your wide smile, your giggle."

"I don't giggle!"

"Yes, you do. And I can hardly wait to hear it in private, but at the moment, we have...company."

Quincee jerked her head around. Gene and Bette, Randolf and the kids hovered on the edge of the

Longacre sidewalk. The children were petting the dog.

As she watched, the Tillotsons strolled toward them, taking an evening walk. No one appeared to be interested in her and Hamilton. Not at all. Only the odd glance happened their way.

"Oh, I do love my neighbors." Quincee sighed.

"So do I," Hamilton said as he kissed her. "So do I."

* * * * *

Dear Reader,

Writing Quincee and Hamilton's story was so much fun. I love the old neighborhoods with the mixed architectural styles, especially when the houses and properties have been lovingly kept by their owners. However, so often in today's rushed world we have little time to get to know our neighbors past a hand wave. Getting involved is a choice we sometimes put aside because of other demands. Yet there are rewards in sitting down to chat over a cup of coffee or over the back fence, too. Mine has been that I remain friends with some of the people with whom I shared a street long ago. Those friendships warm me, and I am grateful for them. I hope you'll take time to chat with your newest neighbor this week—and tell them hello for me.

Ruth Scofield

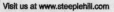

Next Month From Steeple Hill's

Love Inspired

SECRETS OF
THE HEART
by

Gail Gaymer Martin

Social worker Kate Davis finds herself falling for the handsome and charming new doctor in town, Scott Davis. But she's got a secret she's kept hidden for over ten years. Will Kate ever trust in the Lord enough to tell Scott her secret—and give him her heart?

**Don't miss
SECRETS OF THE HEART
On sale August 2001**

Love Inspired

Visit us at www.steeplehill.com
LISOTH

Next month from Steeple Hill's

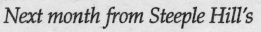

A CHILD
SHALL LEAD THEM
by

Carole Gift Page

Counselor Brianna Rowlands unexpectedly
becomes the legal guardian of a baby girl when a
young woman she counsels falls ill and dies. The
baby's uncle, Eric Wingate, is more than happy to
help find a good home for his niece, but he doesn't
feel ready to raise her by himself. When Eric and
Brianna realize they are falling in love, will they
decide to create a family "made in heaven"?

Don't miss
A CHILD SHALL LEAD THEM
On sale September 2001